The Soldier's Sweetheart

Deb Kastner

⟨H⟩HARLEQUIN® LOVE INSPIRED®

Recycling programs
for this product may
not exist in your area.

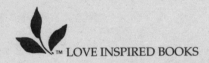 ™ LOVE INSPIRED BOOKS

ISBN-13: 978-0-373-81710-8

THE SOLDIER'S SWEETHEART

Copyright © 2013 by Debra Kastner

www.LoveInspiredBooks.com

Printed in U.S.A.

The Lord your God is with you,
the Mighty Warrior who saves.
He will take great delight in you;
in His love He will no longer rebuke you,
but will rejoice over you with singing.
—*Zephaniah* 3:17

To all the mighty warriors who daily
put their lives on the line to keep our country safe.
Words are not enough to thank you for your service.
God bless you and your families.

Chapter One

Sell Sam's Grocery?

Samantha Howell snorted in outrage and crumpled the fancy-shmancy letter, written on white-linen paper, in her fist.

Over her dead body.

Her stomach tightened into uncomfortable knots, the same as it always did when she heard the name Stay-n-Shop. Didn't these people know what the word *no* meant? Just because they were a large corporation didn't mean they could walk over the little people, did it?

Actually, it kind of did. In fact, that was exactly what it meant. And unfortunately for Samantha, she was the "little people" in question.

Fury kindled in her chest as she flattened the note with her palm. As much as she wanted to toss the missive in the nearest trash can, she knew she needed to keep it. This wasn't the first time she'd heard from this giant bear of a company, but if they had their way, it would be the last. Stay-n-Shop had taken out a ninety-day option on land just inside the southern border of Serendipity. If she didn't sell to them, they'd "have no choice but to pursue permits and zoning" and begin building a store of their own. In short, the big-box store would drive Sam's Grocery out of business.

She chewed absently on her bottom lip as she reread the letter once again, her thoughts buzzing through her head like a swarm of angry wasps.

What was she going to do to save her store? What *could* she do?

"Excuse me, miss?"

The bell rang over the door and a moment later, a man's deep, unfamiliar voice registered in her ear.

"I'm sorry to disturb you. I'm looking for Samantha Howell. I was told I might find her here." His tone was as smooth as honey, with just the hint of a Texas accent.

"I'm..." she started to say, frantically sliding the crumpled letter under the nearby drygoods inventory. Her breath hitched as she met the stranger's uncompromising brown-eyed gaze. She swallowed hard, trying to recover her composure.

"…Samantha Howell."

Having lived her whole life in the small town, it was a rare event for her to not recognize someone. Very few visitors ever came through Serendipity, Texas. The town wasn't even on the state map. She knew nearly every customer who frequented the store by name and could recount their lives down to the most current events.

Even more peculiar, she surmised the man was military, despite the fact that he was in street clothes. The severe set of his shoulders, his trim blond hair and the way he clasped his hands behind his back were dead giveaways. And his tan T-shirt was ironed, with a sharp crease lining each sleeve. Only military guys ironed their T-shirts.

She wondered which branch of the service he was in. Before leaving for Fort Benning for Basic Combat Training, her brother, Seth, had tried to enlighten her on the differences between the branches. At the time, she hadn't really been paying attention. Her brother was always talking about Army this or Army that.

To Samantha, military was military. She appreciated their service to the country, and she hung up her flag every Memorial Day and Fourth of July just like any other homegrown patriot would do, but it had all been lip service, without any truly meaningful connection to her real life.

Once Seth enlisted, that changed.

Now every newscast about the American troops, every update on the radio, was personal. It was frightening. It was family.

Seth.

In a matter of milliseconds, Samantha went from being curious about a handsome stranger to completely panicked over a brother living in consistently deadly conditions. She felt as if she'd been zapped with electricity from an open socket. All thoughts of Stay-n-Shop and her own problems instantly fled.

Was this man here about her brother?

Oh, dear Lord. Not Seth.

As the man's solemn gaze held hers, fear and adrenaline jolted her pulse. Her stomach rose into her throat in stinging, nauseating waves, then plunged back down again like a giant, out-of-control roller coaster.

The stranger's expression was grim, his mouth a thin, straight line slashing across hard, angular features. She could read nothing reassuring in his eyes and horrible scenarios spread like wildfire through her mind.

It couldn't be. Not her brother.

Seth had only entered the Army infantry last year. Immediately after his advanced training, he'd been deployed to Afghanistan, where he was working under extremely dangerous circumstances, with guns and bombs and who knew what else threatening him on a daily basis.

And now this military man had suddenly appeared, asking for her by name. Didn't the Army send a guy out when—

Oh, God, she pleaded silently, her heart pounding in her ears as she gasped for breath. *No, no, no. Dear Lord, please don't let this be about Seth. Please don't let him be wounded.*

Or worse.

Samantha gritted her teeth and shook her head. This couldn't be happening. Not to her sweet, charming baby brother, who'd always been the life of the family.

"Is Seth...?" she started to ask, her raw voice cracking under the strain and tears burning in her eyes. The man wasn't in uniform. Wasn't he supposed to be in uniform? "Where is he? Is he okay?"

Confused, the man's dark blond eyebrows dropped low over his eyes, but then his gaze suddenly widened in comprehension. His throat worked as he searched for words.

"No, ma'am. I mean, yes, ma'am. Seth is fine. That's not why I'm here at all." One side of his mouth twitched with strain as he lifted a hand and shook his head. "I'm sorry I gave you the wrong impression. I can see that I've unintentionally frightened you."

Frightened her? He'd scared her half to death with his sober expression. Her heart was pounding so hard she thought he could probably hear it from where he was standing.

"Seth is enjoying his tour of duty—or, at least, as much as a person can find pleasure in their deployment. He was born for military service, as I'm sure you're well aware. He excels in the infantry."

Relief washed over her in waves. This soldier had seen her brother, and Seth was safe and sound.

Thank You, Lord.

"Actually," the man continued, shifting from one foot to the other and clearing his throat, "Seth *is* why I'm here, although not for the reason you supposed. I assumed…" He cleared his throat again. "Although in Seth's defense, everything happened rather quickly."

Samantha's relief turned to bewilderment.

What had happened quickly? Seth could be airheaded at times, but forgetting to mention he was sending a soldier to their town defied being a card-carrying space cadet, even for him.

"I'm afraid I don't understand." A gross understatement, but a place to start. She leaned forward on her elbows and clasped her hands before her. "Obviously, I'm confused here. Can we begin again?"

The man took a step back and squared his already taut shoulders, as if she'd just invaded his personal space. Or maybe it was a figurative movement, a physical gesture indicating that he was preparing to start their encounter all over again.

"I'm Corporal—er—William Davenport. I've obviously caught you off guard with my arrival." His eyebrows lowered as he tilted his head toward her. "You don't know why I am here, nor were you aware that I was coming."

It wasn't a question, but Samantha shook her head, silently reevaluating the figure of masculinity blocking the stream of sunlight pouring in from the front glass window. "I'm afraid not, Mr. Davenport. I believe I'm at a distinct disadvantage here."

But she was quickly coming up to speed. Seth, easily diverted, had forgotten to call and let her know that his friend was coming to Serendipity to…

What?

Visit? Pass through town on his way elsewhere? Get some country air before returning to active duty?

It's too bad her parents' bed-and-breakfast wasn't up and running yet. If it was a little closer to their grand opening, this soldier might have been their first paying customer.

Now that Seth's safety wasn't an issue, she realized there was more her brother had neglected to mention—like how easy William Davenport was on the eyes. Even the scar marring his upper lip gave credence to his rough-cut masculinity. Her best friends, Alexis and Mary, would turn green with envy when she told them about her encounter with the man. If she could unobtrusively snap a picture of him with her cell phone before he left, even better. Then she'd really be able to rub it in.

"Please, call me Will," the man continued, breaking into her thoughts. "I'm recently retired from active duty—a civilian now."

Will. It was a strong name, fitting for the sturdy man before her. His voice had lowered with his brief explanation, and she had the distinct impression that he was uncomfortable with the civilian status he was declaring.

"I'm here to fill the position you have open."

"I'm sorry?" Samantha queried, so taken aback by his statement that she jerked upright, sending both the dry-goods inventory and her briefly forgotten corporate letter flying. She watched in horror as each piece of paper floated slowly and in what felt like an intentional and deliberate way to the floor—directly in front of Will.

Her chest tightened. Maybe it was silly, but she had her pride, and she didn't like anyone reading her private business. But it had very literally landed at his feet, and there was nothing she could do about it.

It was a given that he had to go and pick up the papers off the floor. What else was there for him to do, since the Stay-n-Shop missive covered the tip of one of his meticulously shined black cowboy boots?

Samantha couldn't tell whether or not he glanced at the letter as he scooped it up. He gave nothing away in his expression and his eyes were dark and unreadable. She fought the urge to reach out and snatch the paper out of his hand, and then decided that would be too obvious a move, calling attention to the fact that she was uncomfortable with him reading the letter. Instead, she stood frozen, her hands fisted at her sides.

Without a single word, he turned and reached for the other piece of paper. Samantha quietly sighed in relief when he placed the grocery inventory over the legal missive. He spent a good deal more time looking at the dry-goods register, which made her almost as uncomfortable as the thought of him looking at the Stay-n-Shop letter.

His lips pursed briefly, his right eyebrow twitching once before his expression returned to stone. Had Samantha looked away even for a second, she would have missed the odd mix of emotions that momentarily registered on his face.

He lifted his gaze from the inventory and took a long look around the store, apparently taking stock of what Sam's Grocery carried, glancing back and forth between the products on the shelves and the list he still carried in his hand.

Was he judging the place? He gave no further indication one way or another of what he was thinking as he perused the shop.

"This is it, then? Your whole dry-goods inventory?" he asked, handing both pages back to Samantha as if they'd been his to begin with. He had a commanding air about him that Samantha didn't particularly care for. She considered herself a friendly and easygoing woman, but when it came to Sam's Grocery, she was used to being in charge, and she certainly wasn't used to being questioned about the state of her dry-goods inventory—especially by a stranger. Add to that the fact that she'd already had a long and stressful afternoon, and she was ripe for contention.

"Yes," she answered brusquely, not that it was any of his business. "So?"

"I am—I mean, I *was*—a unit supply specialist in the Army. I'm not sure how well that experience is going to segue into working for a small-town grocery, but I'll do my best. You'll find I'm quite diligent in my work habits."

"Yeah—about that." She jumped in before he had the opportunity to elaborate on why he was qualified for this job—the one he mistakenly thought was on the table for him, or worse yet, thanks to her capricious brother, believed was already a signed-and-sealed deal. She was still a little unclear on that point. "I'm not quite sure I understand which position, exactly, you think we have open. As you observed, Serendipity is a small town, and this is a family grocery. We don't have much occasion to hire help here."

Clearing his throat, Will glanced behind him. Samantha followed his gaze and thought she saw a slight shadow flitting across the sunshine pouring in through the glass window, but she quickly brushed it off as nothing. It was probably only some animal scavenging for free treats.

"I guessed this was a family-operated business by the name on the sign outside. You're Samantha, the owner of the place and Seth's sister. That's the reason I asked specifically for you."

"Yup, that's me. My parents, Samuel and

Amanda, recently retired and left the grocery to me," Samantha explained. "It's something of a legacy."

"Indeed."

Was he being condescending? Samantha's hackles rose until she met his earnest gaze—not warm, by any means, but sincere and intense.

"And do you do this all by yourself, or do you have other employees?"

"I have a woman who comes in and prepares the fresh deli products—you know, potato salad and cooked hens and the like. We sell baked goods acquired by the local café. My parents come in a couple of days a week to help out." She gestured to the rest of the store. "Other than that, you're looking at her—manager, stocker, cashier and bag-person," she said, relaxing a little. Maybe if she smiled at him he'd lose some of the somber tension from his face.

Smiles were supposed to be viral, right?

"Seth spoke of you often," Will commented in the rich, quiet manner that Samantha was beginning to realize was his normal tone of voice—not at all what she'd expect from an Army guy, based on what she knew of her brother.

"I'm sorry I can't say the same," Samantha said, regarding Will with new eyes. "Unfortunately, Seth neglected to mention you."

"He said you work too hard and never get

a break, and frankly, he's worried about you. That's part of the reason I'm here—to take some of that burden from you."

As he spoke, Samantha noticed that Will's lips naturally turned down at the corners—they didn't lend themselves to an easy grin.

"Seth and I realized we could assist each other in what could possibly be an advantageous relationship for both of us," he continued. "Besides, you know your brother—once he gets something in his mind, it's hard to convince him otherwise." Will shrugged one shoulder. "So here I am."

"I see," she replied, though in truth, she didn't. The way Will was speaking, it almost sounded like he was here against his better judgment.

It was definitely against Samantha's. She wished Seth was here so she could knock him in the head. What was he thinking, sending someone who was probably a slap-happy, risk-taking adrenaline junkie to fill what was, for the most part, a repetitive and predictable position?

A *slow* job. Not that an employment opportunity really existed, but even if it did, nothing in Serendipity moved fast, nor did it change much from day to day. She couldn't imagine how Will would adapt to such sluggish surroundings.

Wasn't that part of the reason Seth had enlisted in the Army in the first place? To remove himself from a situation that would have eventually bored him to tears or sent him to the insane asylum? Samantha couldn't see how he expected that Will would fare much better. This soldier had seen combat. Working day in and day out in the grocery would be the polar opposite.

But maybe that was the point. Maybe that was exactly what Will was looking for. Someplace quiet to get away from the memories of war.

Great. *Now* how was she going to politely turn the man away? Like she didn't have enough problems already, trying to deal with the ever-increasing threat of a big-box takeover.

The bell rang over the door and her parents entered, their faces eager with anticipation. They rushed forward all at once in a gibber of exclamations, trying to be heard over each other to be the first to welcome Will to Serendipity.

Samantha reached for the Stay-n-Shop missive and tucked it under the counter.

"You must be William," her mother said, stepping forward to embrace the poor man, who looked dreadfully uncomfortable with the public show of affection. He froze at attention like a statue, his arms stiff at his sides.

Her mother, with bountiful curves and a frizzy head of blond hair, was a good foot shorter than Will. At her tallest, she didn't even reach the middle of his chest, but that didn't stop her from exclaiming loudly and squeezing him in what others might consider an excessively friendly manner.

To Samantha, it was just her mother being her usual outgoing, jovial self, not noticing how uneasy she was making Will and chattering on as if nothing was amiss. "Seth has told us all about you. We're so delighted you'll be staying with us."

Seth had told *them* about Will? And he'd be *staying* with them?

Two more shockers in a long day full of them.

Just lovely. Not only had Seth somehow arranged for Will to have a job at the grocery— apparently with her parents' knowledge and concurrence, and without a word to her—but now he'd be staying with them, whatever that meant.

Happily, whatever they were referring to, it didn't involve her, not directly anyway, since she lived in her own apartment close to the store. Her parents' house was empty most of the time, as they were working on their retirement dreams—building a bed-and-breakfast. They'd recently purchased some land along a gentle creek and were renovating several old cottages situated close to the water, but the cabins weren't yet ready for habitation. Seth's room was vacant, but surely her brother would never agree to such an arrangement. Many of his personal belongings were still in that room, untouched, souvenirs from his boyhood saved like a time capsule for when he was home on leave.

"It's good to meet you, son," her father said, extending his hand to Will.

"Thank you, sir," Will answered, clearly more comfortable with her dad's welcome than that of her over-affectionate mother.

"It's Samuel," her father corrected in his typical booming bass. "And my wife here is Amanda. The only 'sir' around these parts is my pop, Grandpa Sampson, whom you'll meet later, after you've settled in. We're glad you're here, and we're grateful to God for your help, both in the store and with our cabins. They're in dire need of repair before we can offer them to guests."

"I'm happy to be able to help you folks out and appreciate your offer of lodging, at least until I can get permanently settled."

So that's what it was, then. Room and board in exchange for his carpentry skills. Not such a bad idea, though she still wondered why no one had bothered to mention to *her* that Will was going to show up at her doorstep and demand a job.

Okay, maybe that was putting it a little harshly. Will hadn't exactly burst in and *demanded* a job. More like he'd simply assumed it was there—which, apparently, it was.

A simple "you've got a gorgeous ex-Army guy coming to work for you" would have been nice.

Samantha chuckled at her private joke. After the day she'd had, she either had to laugh or she was going to burst into tears. This was a lot to take in, and in a short time, too.

She pinched her lips, fighting the emotion surging through her chest, trying to sort out the mixed-up messages her heart was sending her brain and working not to give in to the indignant sense of betrayal she was experiencing.

Had everyone purposely kept her in the dark?

That stung more than she cared to admit. Why would her brother—never mind her parents—keep something this momentous from her? Did they not trust her? Did they think she wouldn't welcome Will with open arms?

She glanced at her parents, now speaking in soft tones with Will, and wondered if anyone would miss her if she slipped out of the store for a few minutes. She needed to vent to someone, preferably Alexis and Mary, whom she was certain would see her side of this situation.

She pulled out her cell phone and used her

thumbs as she texted: *Gorgeous ex-Army guy just walked in.*

That should pique their curiosity. If she knew Alexis and Mary, they'd show up at the grocery faster in the hopes of meeting an eligible bachelor than if she'd told them it was a 911 emergency.

She gazed toward the glass door, focusing on the sunshine. The sun always reminded her of her faith and it generally gave her peace.

And it did, for a moment, until she caught the hint of movement from behind the candy aisle—and an adorable little girl appeared.

Will followed Samantha's gaze to where his four-year-old daughter, Genevieve, was peeking out from behind the candy aisle. All he could see of Genevieve from where he was standing was the thick mop of black curls that she had inherited from her mother and the large, inquisitive brown eyes that were very much a reflection of his own.

The scene would have been cute, he supposed, from virtually any other person's vantage point—a curious yet clearly shy little girl hanging back to see how the adults responded before announcing her presence.

She was a little darling, and she stole Will's heart every time he looked at her, but the little girl's gaze also caused him a moment of sheer panic.

He was this child's *father*. She depended entirely upon him, and he hadn't given her any reassurance in this new and unfamiliar situation.

His throat closed and burned from the effort of withholding the onslaught of emotion. It was difficult to breathe, and his pulse roared in his head. Shame burned his cheeks. In all the confusion, he'd forgotten to introduce Genevieve.

She'd held back when they'd first entered, and he'd allowed her to stay near the door, thinking it would be easier for her if he served as point man. He supposed he'd expected her to come forward once he'd introduced himself to the management, so to speak.

Instead, she'd hidden in an aisle and stayed there—probably waiting for him to reassure her that everything was all right.

Which, to his chagrin, he had not done.

She was a furtive little thing—Seth's parents hadn't even seen her when they'd entered the store. But that was no excuse on his part.

This was not at all the impression he was trying to create with the Howells right off the bat, and most certainly not the way he wanted to treat his daughter. The fact that he *felt* entirely incompetent as a father was one thing. But he didn't need to display his inadequacies for the whole world to see.

Meeting Seth's older sister had really thrown him for a loop. Seth was a good-looking kid, so it should have been no surprise to him that his sister was an attractive woman. Samantha had straight, thick black hair cut in an appealing pixie style that showed off the endearing curl of her ears. She shared her brother's enormous cobalt-blue eyes, but they were breathtaking on Samantha.

Will cleared his throat and stepped over to his daughter, awkwardly placing a hand on her shoulder as he gently urged her from her hiding place.

"Folks, this is my daughter, Genevieve."

Genevieve immediately slid behind him, clutching at his legs and peering out at the unfamiliar people from behind his right knee. He crouched and picked her up in his arms. "Say hi to the nice folks."

"Hi." Genevieve said the word because her daddy had asked her to, but she didn't sound convinced that she should be speaking to strangers.

"May your daughter have a lollipop?" Samantha asked, coming out from behind the counter. He turned and met her gaze. Was this a trick question? Was he supposed to decline and ask for an apple instead? What would a *good* father do in this situation?

"I—uh," he floundered.

"She's not allergic, is she?"

"No. I mean, I don't think so." How was he supposed to keep his daughter safe if he didn't know vital things about her? He could accidentally put her in jeopardy without ever realizing he was doing so.

"Then perhaps just this once, since it's such a special occasion."

Will nodded, relief flooding through him. It was as if Samantha had somehow guessed that he hadn't known how to answer her and was filling in the blanks for him. He was grateful for her assistance.

Then again, she had put just the slightest emphasis on the words *special occasion*. He had the distinct feeling Samantha was a little miffed at him. It wasn't his fault she hadn't known he was coming. She could point that finger at her brother.

"Hey, Genevieve," Samantha said in a considerably sweeter, gentler tone of voice than she had used with Will. "Do you want to pick out a lollipop from the jar over there?"

She held out her hands, and to Will's surprise, Genevieve slid into her arms without the slightest bit of fuss. The little girl's eyes were still wide with a mixture of curiosity and hesitation, but she allowed Samantha to carry her to the candy jar. Samantha set Genevieve on the counter and lifted the lid so she could select the flavor of her choice.

Genevieve immediately picked purple. Grape. Will filed the information in his mind. Knowing Genevieve's preferences might come in handy, especially if he was ever asked to choose something in his daughter's stead—which he was beginning to realize was going come up more often than he could even imagine.

Clothes for school. Dresses. Shoes. Hair bows. What did he know about raising a little girl?

Nothing. Not a single thing.

Haley would have been able to pick out a lollipop for Genevieve. For all he knew, grape had also been Haley's favorite.

He realized to his chagrin that he didn't know *what* flavor his wife had preferred when she was alive. There were a lot of things he hadn't taken the time to find out about Haley, and now it was too late to rectify his oversights, to make right all the many ways he'd erred as a husband.

He cringed and squared his shoulders. Maybe it was too late to change the way things had gone down with Haley, but he could still be a good father to Genevieve, and that was exactly what he was going to do—make it up to her for the years he'd been away, and never let her feel alone or unprotected again.

It was his one resolution in life—to make things right with his daughter.

"You want one?" Samantha asked, holding the candy bowl out to him. "It's on me. Free of charge."

Belatedly he realized he'd been staring at her and his composure nearly dropped. Only his many years of military training kept him from showing the apprehension that he felt in his gut.

For a moment, he'd actually considered taking the candy. He couldn't remember the last time he'd tasted a lollipop. Maybe not since early childhood. But he wasn't a kid anymore.

"No, but thank you for offering," he answered after an extended pause.

"She's a lovely little girl," Amanda Howell said. "Seth mentioned you're a single father?"

"Yes, ma'am." Will's throat felt scratchy and raw as he answered. "Genevieve's mother passed away about four months back. My daughter stayed with my in-laws until my tour of duty was up, but now I'm looking to be a full-time daddy to her."

"We'll help you as much as we can," Amanda assured him. "Isn't that right, Samantha?"

"Hmm?" Samantha was entertaining Genevieve and clearly hadn't heard her mother's declaration.

"I was just telling Will how we'd help him out with his sweet little girl," her mother repeated. "You're especially good with children. Genevieve has already taken to you."

Samantha's blue eyes widened as she looked from her mother to Genevieve and back again. Then her gaze turned to Will. "I think my mom is referring to me teaching the preschool and kindergarten Sunday school classes at church," she explained, shrugging one shoulder.

Teaching preschool and kindergarten. Those were pretty good credentials, as far as Will was concerned. As long as she didn't press Genevieve too hard on spiritual matters, she might really be the help he needed.

If she wanted to help him. Considering the way her mother appeared to be pushing him on her, Will wasn't so certain about that fact.

The bell rang over the door and everyone turned at once. Two women—one with windswept brown hair and green eyes, the other with long, straight blond hair pulled back in a ponytail—whirled into the place like a couple of dervishes on a mission.

"We came as soon as we heard," the blond said, flicking her ponytail as she made her way straight for Will. "This must be the handsome guy you texted us about. And an ex-soldier, no less. Whew!"

Will looked at Samantha. She'd texted her friends about him? Maybe she wasn't as put off by his appearance as she'd first appeared to be. In any case, she was definitely embarrassed now. Her face was bright scarlet, the poor woman, at the uncomfortable spot her friend had just placed her in.

Of course, they'd placed him in as equally tight a spot.

"My name is Alexis Granger. *Very* glad to meet you," the blonde purred, holding out a hand for him to shake. She had a firm grip, not one of those faint finger-shakes so many women were fond of. She was dusty and dressed for riding, and Will could smell what he guessed must be horses, a distinct and peculiar scent to which his nose wasn't accustomed.

It wasn't bad, exactly. Just different. And it was just one of a million and one ways he'd discovered so far today how dissimilar Serendipity was from the big-city and military lifestyle he'd known in the past.

"I'm Mary," the brunette said with shy nod. "Welcome to Serendipity." At least she didn't invade his personal space, although there was no doubt that she was eyeing him appreciatively. Between Samantha's two friends, Will was starting to feel like the candy in that jar Samantha was holding.

"I'm William Davenport," he said, shaking Mary's hand. Her grip was softer than Alexis's, more delicate. "Please call me Will."

"Will is going to be staying in Serendipity," Samantha explained. Her voice sounded high and strained to Will's ears.

Both of her friends exclaimed in delight and high-fived each other. Didn't they realize he was standing right here watching them?

Hello. Still in the room.

Mary and Alexis circled Samantha and launched into a garble of speech, but it was difficult for Will to make out what they were saying—and not because they were speaking in whispered tones.

Oh, no. Quite the opposite. They were chattering away like chickens in a henhouse, their voices high and staccato. Samantha held her hands up in protest and rolled her eyes.

Didn't these people ever have visitors in their town? Or was it just the fact that he was a presumably single man that piqued their interest?

If that was what they were excited about, they were in for an enormous disappointment. Will wasn't the least bit interested in a relationship here in Serendipity. He was here to work, and to get to know his little girl—and that was it.

No more. No less.

He'd already messed up one woman's life with his attention—or lack thereof. He wouldn't do it again.

"We were just discussing where Will and Genevieve will be living," Amanda interjected, her voice a surprisingly reasonable, even tone compared to the younger women.

And he'd thought *she* was overly exuberant when he'd first met her.

"If he needs a place to stay, there's plenty of room on my ranch," Alexis offered with a flirtatious grin. "You could kick back with the stable hands. They've got a few extra bunks."

"I'd invite you," said Mary, her cheeks coloring a rose pink, "except that I live alone."

"You're not exactly alone with those gazillion dogs of yours," Alexis amended with a hoot.

Mary chuckled. "What about asking Pastor Shawn for assistance?"

"Ladies," Samuel said, toning down the conversation like a maestro controlling a symphony. "We've already got the details of Will's living arrangements worked out to everyone's satisfaction. He'll be staying in one of our cabins along the creek and doing cabinetry work for us in exchange for room and board. Everybody wins."

Samantha sputtered and looked like she was choking. Her face turned beet red and her mouth moved, but no words came out. Clearly, she didn't believe *everybody* in this situation would win, but she caught herself and smiled at him.

Will clamped down on the emotions welling in his chest. She had no idea what her help meant to him. It wasn't easy for him to humble his pride and accept assistance, but this wasn't about him. It was about Genevieve, and he would do anything for his little girl.

With all he'd been through in the past months, *appreciation* didn't even begin to cover what he owed the Howells for their goodwill. He didn't know how to express it in words.

What he *could* do was pull his weight around here. He could shoulder some of the burden the grocery created. And he could get the B&B cabins into working condition and help the elder Howells realize their dreams.

"I'll get moved into the cabin tonight, and then I'm ready to start work first thing in the morning," he told Samantha.

Her eyebrows rose in surprise. "Tomorrow? Tomorrow is Sunday."

"Right," he agreed. "So?"

"So...the grocery isn't open on Sundays."

"Not at all?"

"Nope. The whole town rolls up at about six o'clock every night and all day on Sundays. You won't find much of anything open around here during the evenings and half of the weekend. Serendipity is an old-fashioned town with old-fashioned ways."

Will whistled through his teeth. "What do people do if they forget an ingredient for Sunday dinner?"

Samantha laughed. "Borrow from their neighbors or make do with what they have on hand. You'll get used to it after a while."

"I sincerely doubt that," Will muttered under his breath. As if he didn't have enough to deal with, now he was living in a town that not only *looked* like a throwback to the late 1800s but acted like it, as well.

"You're welcome to come to church with us tomorrow morning," Samantha offered. "It's a community congregation. You'll have the opportunity to meet a lot of the townspeople."

"No thanks," he said abruptly, and then realized how bad that sounded. These people had been gracious to him. He cleared his throat. "That is to say, I'm not really much of a church-going man. I appreciate the offer, though."

Samantha looked stunned and a little wounded, which surprised him.

"I'll be meeting most of the town folks here at the grocery, won't I?" he asked, in what he hoped was a more positive tone of voice.

"Certainly. Of course. You can meet people

here at the store." Samantha smiled, though it didn't quite reach her eyes.

He hadn't meant to hurt her feelings, but surely he wasn't the only man in town who didn't believe in a feel-good deity who handed out free favors, or worse yet, an angry God who zapped people with bolts of lightning when He didn't like what they were doing.

If he was going to believe in one of those, it would surely be the latter. His life hadn't been graced with many favors.

But then again, if there was a God who punished people for their sins, he would have been deep-fried a long time ago.

Somehow, he thought there was probably more to Samantha's request to join them at church tomorrow than just meeting folks from town. But now that he'd turned her down, he would never know.

Chapter Two

Sunday was Samantha's only real day off. As she'd informed Will, Sam's Grocery, like every other shop in town, was closed on Sundays. After she spent the morning playing the organ for the church and sharing a nice family dinner with her parents, Sunday afternoon was her time to kick back and relax, maybe read a romance novel or watch some television.

But today was a sunny day, and Samantha decided she didn't want to stay indoors. Problems were plaguing her and she desperately needed some fresh air to clear her head.

Her first inclination was to go find her friends. She was certain that Mary and Alexis had plenty to say about Will. They'd probably already started making plans for landing him a wife here in Serendipity, possibly even tossing a coin as to which one of them would have the honor.

But Samantha didn't really want to talk about Will. She didn't even want to think about him, though unfortunately, she couldn't seem to get him out of her head. She was still mildly resentful of the fact that he'd had been thrust into her life with no notice.

Still, thinking about Will was preferable to thinking about her other issue—the letter from Stay-n-Shop. She still had no idea how she was going to handle that matter.

She sighed. One problem at a time.

Since Will was on her mind anyway, maybe she could do something nice for him and Genevieve. Take them to the park, maybe?

She raised her head and smiled, making a conscious decision to put her fears aside for the day and concentrate on her faith. This was Sunday, after all.

Despite her reservations about her new employee, she didn't have a heart of stone, and the guy had his plate full trying to take care of his little girl on his own. She had the impression he was determined to do his best despite the reticence she thought she sensed in him.

And Genevieve—the poor sweetheart, losing her mother at such a tender young age. Samantha had had a wonderful childhood with two parents who loved her and each other, and paternal grandparents who'd been married, well, forever, until her grandmother had passed away at age seventy-five last year. She couldn't imagine what losing a mother must feel like—especially for a four-year-old.

Samantha didn't know the specifics of how Genevieve's mother had died, but she knew enough to know that the little girl was both frightened and confused by her new surroundings, and by suddenly having to live with a father she hardly knew.

Yesterday at the shop, Genevieve hadn't smiled—not even when she was enticed with candy. Not even when her father picked her up in his arms. She'd barely spoken more than a word, though Samantha had encouraged her every way she knew how.

Did the child have some disability, or had recent circumstances and emotional issues just caused her to hide in her shell? She supposed only time would tell.

It didn't help that Will wasn't sure of himself as a father. Despite how strong he appeared upon first observation, she'd glimpsed the buck-in-the-headlights look when his eyes alighted on his daughter. That he loved her was evident. That he wasn't sure what to do with her was equally evident. Samantha didn't think he was as hopeless as he believed himself to be, but again, only time would tell on that count.

God had laid a lot on her plate in the past day. Will was here to stay, and somehow, she had to find a way to integrate him into her daily life. Like *that* was going to be easy. There was plenty of work to be done, and in truth Samantha was intrigued by the idea of having help, but not from the large, handsome ex-soldier.

She suspected he would be more of a hindrance than a help. Really, how could he not be? His size alone would be a hindrance—he'd be bumping into things all over the place. Besides, the store could only be described as slow and steady and the work was repetitive, with little beyond the daily routine to break up the monotony. He'd be bored one day into the job, and in her experience, bored men meant trouble.

Like her brother, for example, who couldn't keep an inventory straight to save his life, not because he couldn't count, but because he got sidetracked by every pretty girl who entered the store.

She sighed and reminded herself again that this was not a day for problems. She didn't have the slightest idea what she was going to do with Will, but at least she had some idea of what to do with his daughter.

She walked up to the cottage door where Will and Genevieve were staying and paused a moment to collect herself. It wouldn't do for Will to see that she was still struggling with her own feelings of frustration and resentment. Those were her issues, not his.

She knew that God would want her to be generous and charitable—but knowing the truth and feeling it were two different things entirely. Sometimes a woman just had to live by faith and wait for her heart to catch up to her.

She took a deep breath and knocked.

No one answered, so after a moment, she knocked again, harder this time.

"Hello," she called. "Anybody home? It's Samantha." She thought about peering in the front window but decided it would be rude and might invade his privacy.

She'd just reached out to knock a third time when the door flew open and she nearly fell into the room. Will stood in the entrance holding Genevieve. The girl was wrapped in a green bath towel with a froggie face on the hood. Wet black curls framed her face and water dripped from her nose.

Will looked as if he'd taken a dunk. He was wearing worn blue jeans and an Army-issue tan T-shirt that was soaked with water, clinging to his chest and muscular arms. She couldn't help but take a second look.

Samantha held back a chuckle when she realized he had bath bubbles clinging to the spiked blond hair on top of his head.

"You…uh…" she said, pointing awkwardly, "have…"

Instead of finishing her sentence, she reached up on tiptoe and scooped the bubbles into her palm. With a playful grin, she held them out to him so he could see.

"A new fashion statement?" she teased.

She thought that would bring a laugh—or at the very least a smile—but instead his expression darkened.

"I was trying to give Genevieve a bath," he explained, as if it wasn't perfectly obvious. "As you can see, my mission was an epic fail."

Samantha smothered another laugh. Only an Army guy would consider giving his child a bath a *mission*. And how did one *fail* a bath, anyway?

Her gaze swept over Genevieve. "She looks clean enough to me."

Will sighed. "Maybe. But you should see the state of the bathroom." He gestured at his shirt-front. "Also, I hadn't intended to give *myself* a bath in the process."

Samantha made a final, valiant effort not to laugh at what Will clearly did not consider to be a humorous situation, but this time, a chuckle sputtered from her lips.

He looked at his shirtfront and then back at her, his twinkling chocolate-colored gaze mixing with hers. Her breath hitched.

"This is funny, isn't it?"

"Well…yeah. Pretty much. Cute, too."

"Cute?" He choked out the word, clearly appalled by the notion.

"I meant Genevieve," she assured him, though in all honesty, Will, with his wet clothes and bath bubbles in his hair, was every bit as adorable as his little girl.

Which was precisely what Samantha suspected a man's man like Will Davenport would *not* want to know about himself.

There was no doubt in Samantha's mind that every unmarried woman in Serendipity—except for her, of course—was going to be doing all she could to catch Will's eye. Will was going to have his work cut out for him.

"I came by to see if you and Genevieve might like to join me for a picnic in the park." She lofted the picnic basket she carried in her left hand. "I've got ham, turkey, fresh rolls, some fruit and cheese. I wasn't sure what you liked, so I threw in a little bit of everything."

He eyed the basket speculatively and then shook his head. "Thanks for the offer, but I think Genevieve might feel overwhelmed playing at a park with a bunch of kids she doesn't know."

"Is she normally shy around other children?"

He frowned. "I don't know."

"Well, then, there's no harm in trying, is there? If she's not enjoying herself, we can always bring her back home. But I suspect she may surprise you."

He glanced behind him, as if remembering something important he had forgotten to do. "I've still got a lot to accomplish to get us settled in before I start work in the morning."

She could hear the hesitation in his voice, but she couldn't tell if it was because he felt a duty to get his things in order, or because he didn't want to go with her and was searching for a polite way to decline her invitation.

"Oh, come on," she urged. "You have to eat."

"I'm hungry," announced Genevieve.

Will's gaze met Samantha's and they both chuckled. He tapped the tip of his daughter's nose. "Well, then, Monkey," he said, reaching to take the picnic basket from Samantha, "I guess we'd better get you dressed so Miss Howell can take us to the park."

Leaning on one elbow, Will stretched his legs out on the picnic blanket and popped a bit of a fresh whole-wheat roll into his mouth, savoring the way it melted on his tongue. The roll was perfectly baked, just the way he liked it—crispy outside and soft inside.

Samantha, Will was quickly learning, was a lot like the bread she'd brought—a little hard on the outside, at least upon first meeting, but a real softy inside.

Samantha shrieked playfully as Genevieve chased her. The little girl was, as Samantha had predicted, having a wonderful time in the park, both with the other children and with Samantha, who at first hovered protectively nearby without making Genevieve feel uncomfortable, and then flat-out joined in the games.

The kids accepted Samantha as if she was one of their own, as if it wasn't odd to see an adult crawling through their tunnels and climbing over the bars on their jungle gym. They laughed and played alongside her, even giving her a turn on the slide when she asked.

Will watched with amusement as Samantha worked up a little too much speed sliding down and, with a screech of surprise, landed on her backside, creating a cloud of dust in the sand.

Will was on his feet in an instant, offering her a hand up.

"That looked like it hurt," he commented as she brushed the sand from her jeans.

She beamed at him, her blue eyes sparkling.

"The only ache is my dignity, and I don't have much of that to begin with."

Her lack of self-consciousness made Will a little jealous. He'd spent his whole life striving for decorum and honor, and yet he knew perfectly well that he had failed in every way possible to be a man. He'd never been able to please his own father. He hadn't been a good husband and father himself. He'd hurt the people he'd professed to love. Besides that, he wasn't ignorant of the fact that, with his naturally pessimistic personality, he came off as a regular old sourpuss, whereas Samantha, with seemingly effortless ease and grace, laughed at the world—and more importantly, at herself—and was a better person for it.

Though it pained him to admit it, he clearly had a lot to learn from the woman.

Genevieve ran up and tugged on the bottom of his shirt. "Swing me, swing me, Daddy," she begged, smiling up at him.

Smiling.

That hadn't happened much in the little girl's life lately. She hadn't had much to smile about.

Will's heart melted right there on the spot. What a beautiful child she was. He could see her mother in her, but what really choked him up was that he could see himself in her, as well.

How had such a lovely little thing come from a soul as ugly as his?

"All right, Monkey," he agreed. "Let's go swing." He lifted her into his arms and headed for the swing set. He intended to deposit her into one of the safety swings, the ones with four sides and holes for the legs.

"No, Daddy," Genevieve protested. "I want to swing on the big-girl swing."

Will glanced at Samantha, hoping she'd give him some much-needed direction. He didn't want to make the wrong decision and end up hurting his daughter.

"Yeah. Come on, Dad. The big-girl swing," Samantha echoed with a laugh.

Will realized that what he'd really wanted was Samantha to back him up on the decision he had already made, not agree with Genevieve. He was loath to admit that he was scared half out of his wits that his daughter would lose her balance and fall to the ground.

If she got hurt, it was all on him.

Both Samantha and Genevieve were looking at him expectantly, waiting for his decision. He didn't see any way out of it now. He was good and stuck. He set his jaw as he perched Genevieve on the *big-girl* swing, waiting until she had a good hold on the chains before giving her a gentle push.

"Higher, Daddy. Higher!"

"Honey, I don't know if that's a good idea," Will responded, once again glancing at Samantha for support, sure that she'd back him up on this one. Genevieve was so little, and the swing so high. It was a long way to fall.

Samantha laid a hand on his shoulder. "It's okay," she assured him. "Don't you remember when you were a little kid, what a thrill you got from swinging just as high as you could?"

Will cringed. He couldn't remember much from his own childhood, at least not much that he cared to recall. He knew he hadn't had a lot of playground time, not even when he was young. He'd had a strict father who believed children should be busy working for the food they ate. His father had never been happy with Will's performance, no matter how hard he'd tried.

The memory of his father's bitter voice echoed through his head. *You can't go to church. Church is for good people. You are not good.* Will had spent all his time doing chores and studying for school and dreaming of the moment he'd be old enough to leave that house permanently.

The day he'd turned eighteen, he'd enlisted in the U.S. Army, and he hadn't ever looked back.

He wasn't going to let his daughter feel that way about *her* life.

With a whoop and a smile, he pulled Genevieve back and pushed, giving her the freedom to fly.

Chapter Three

"Yes. No. Maybe so." Genevieve repeated the words Samantha had taught her, a game she and her brother had played as a child. The little girl's high-pitched laughter pealed through the otherwise silent store, and Samantha's heartbeat rose in crescendo. She'd really grown to care for the little girl in the days since Will and Genevieve had so suddenly entered her life.

Samantha held Genevieve around the waist as the girl perched on the counter in Sam's Grocery and swung her feet in rhythm to the chant. Since it was summer, Genevieve was staying with Samantha's parents while Samantha and Will worked in the store, but the older couple had come into town to pick up some supplies from the hardware store and had dropped the girl off for a quick visit with her papa.

Samantha thought perhaps Will would join in

the fun, but he just leaned his shoulder against the back wall, crossed his arms, and silently observed, his expression as unreadable as always. He was either angry about something or bored out of his skull. For all his glowering, Samantha had found Will to be a kind and soft-spoken man, so she guessed it was the latter.

Genevieve was clearly an expert at amusing herself and had quickly picked up on the game. Taking her cue from Samantha, she nodded, then shook her head and then shrugged offhandedly as she repeated the phrase over and over again, laughing all the more as her voice echoed throughout the store.

"Yes. No. Maybe so."

"Practicing to be a grown woman, Monkey?" Will asked, walking to the counter and ruffling his daughter's curly black hair affectionately.

Samantha practically did a double take. Had he cracked a joke? That would be a first. Will rarely spoke, and even when he did, he was solemn both in word and expression. Samantha sensed a golden opportunity here to draw him out of his shell a bit.

"Hey, now," she protested. "Watch it there, mister. You're in the company of a *grown woman*. You're going to get in trouble if you keep talking that way."

Will's left eyebrow darted upward. He wasn't

smiling, exactly, but the corner of his mouth moved just a little. "Just sayin'."

Samantha sniffed in feigned offense. "No comment."

At least it appeared he was trying, which was enormous, not only for his own sake, but for his daughter's. Genevieve needed a father who could let go and laugh once in a while. Will wouldn't be qualifying as a stand-up comic any time soon, but his jest was more lighthearted than anything else she'd ever heard from him. It was progress.

"What have we got on our agenda today?" Will asked, his expression fading into the serious demeanor Samantha now associated with him, the creases around his eyes and over his forehead deepening as his brows lowered.

"Not much," she answered, nodding her head toward the stockroom. "We've got a few boxes of canned vegetables to put out on the shelves. If you feel so inclined, you can give everything a good dusting before you place the product." She reached under the counter and grabbed a large ostrich-feather duster, waving it like a flag on the Fourth of July.

The look on his face was priceless, somewhere between pure surprise and utter mortification.

"You want me to dust with that?" he choked out.

"Is that a problem for you?"

"No." He answered too fast, clearly backpedaling. "It's just that…"

She raised a brow.

"I am going to look ridiculous using a feather duster. Do you want me to wear a frilly apron, as well?"

"Like a fifties housewife, you mean?"

He coughed. If it was anyone but Will, Samantha might have mistaken it for a laugh. "Yeah. Exactly like that."

She laughed, reached under the counter again and tossed a rag at him. "Better?"

"Much," he agreed, shifting from one foot to another and rustling the tips of his hair with his free hand. His lips pursed as he glanced from Samantha to Genevieve and back. She had the notion that he wanted to say something more, but he turned away without a word.

The man was already getting antsy. How on earth was she going to keep him busy? He was used to an exciting, fast-paced military lifestyle, not front-facing cans of green beans on a grocery shelf.

"I'll bring out the boxes of vegetables then." Without another word, he moved into the back room. She could hear him stacking boxes of cans onto a cart, and after a moment, he brought them to the shelves.

Samantha continued to play with Genevieve. She was glad to see the little girl coming out of her shell. School would be starting soon. The small, close-knit Serendipity classroom might be exactly what the girl needed to help her get past the trauma she'd experienced with her mother's death. Samantha hoped so, for Will's sake as well as Genevieve's.

She served the few customers who came and went, greeting each by name and asking about their lives. Often she could guess what they'd come in after without them having to say. That was what it was like living and working in Serendipity, and a big part of what Samantha loved about serving people as the grocery manager.

To her surprise, Will enjoyed speaking to the folks who'd stopped by. Though she'd expected him to be ruffled by the intimacy, the small-town dynamic didn't appear to be affecting him at all. He greeted everyone who came through the store with a friendly smile, taking the time to introduce himself and relay the brief story of how he came to be in Serendipity. Oddly, he didn't seem to mind repeating the tale over and over again.

Folks were curious, and Samantha knew that by the end of this week, if they didn't know already, most of the town would be aware she had a new employee. She was certain Mary and

Alexis had already spread the word, igniting interest in the handsome, quiet, *widowed* soldier. Once the news reached Jo Spencer—the woman who ran the local café, and the town's biggest gossip—the blaze would turn into a wildfire. She'd have to fight off the horde of single women who'd be lining up at the door to the shop, making up reasons to visit the grocery while waiting for Will to notice them. There had already been more than a few who'd come in with nothing more than a pack of chewing gum on their lists.

Well, maybe Will would be good for business. Samantha snorted and gave her head a quick shake. That kind of business she really didn't need, but she supposed beggars couldn't be choosers.

At the moment, any business was good business, however it came about.

Thoughts of Stay-n-Shop loomed in her mind, but Samantha pushed them back. She was still praying about what course of action to take on that matter. She didn't have a lot of time, but she knew better than to act rashly without first seeking God's wisdom in the Word and in prayer.

What do I do, Lord? Please make Your will clear to me.

Those were the same words she'd silently repeated dozens of times over the past week, and she knew she was running out of time. *Make Your will known.*

It wasn't long before Samantha's parents stopped by and picked up Genevieve, and the store seemed too quiet without the little girl around. Odd, since before Will and Genevieve, she'd often been the only one in the grocery. She'd never noticed the silence before.

Samantha hunkered over the dry-goods inventory—the one she hadn't finished on Saturday due to Will's arrival—looking up only when one of her neighbors, Delia Bowden, appeared outside the door. Delia's right arm was laden with her newborn daughter, Faith, in an infant car seat while she managed her active toddler, James, with the other.

Delia usually brought her teenage son, Riley, to help out with the groceries, but today he was nowhere to be seen. No big surprise, Samantha supposed. The boy was getting to that age where he didn't want to be seen shopping with his mother.

Will opened the door for Delia, welcoming her into the store with a smile and procuring a cart for her so she could set Faith's car seat in the front. Samantha was still marveling at the way he turned into a different person when he was around the customers. It was odd—and unsettling—that he could turn the charm on and off like a light switch. Especially since it was usually *off* around her.

"Hey, Will?" she called, waving him forward.

He strode toward her, his smile disappearing. She was beginning to wonder if he just didn't like her. It wasn't that she thought he was purposefully trying to hurt her feelings, but she wasn't sure how she would be able to keep working with him every day if he didn't lighten up a bit. Her heart wasn't made of stone. And it *did* hurt.

"As you can see, Delia has her hands full with her kiddos," she said, gesturing to the woman and her children.

"Yeah. I noticed."

"It would be a great kindness to her if you could help her with her shopping."

"Help her?" He shook his head. "I'm not sure I understand what you're saying. I already got her a cart."

"I noticed. It was very thoughtful of you. I was thinking you could, you know, push the cart for her, retrieve groceries from the shelves, especially the high ones. Just give her a hand in general—whatever she needs."

"Wow," he said, whistling under his breath. He almost smiled at her. "Talk about customer service."

Samantha laughed. "That's how we do it in the country. Up close and personal."

"I'll say." Now he was teasing her. Honestly! The man was jerking her strings. "As I'm sure you're becoming increasingly aware, everything is more difficult with children in tow."

"Tell me about it. I can't seem to get anything done when Genevieve is with me. It's all I can do just to keep up with her."

There it was. Finally. A real half smile. He shrugged one shoulder and strode toward Delia and her children, and offered his assistance with a grin.

Samantha's breath caught in her throat. Will was quite attractive when he relaxed—which he never seemed to do around her.

"You're staring," said a high-pitched voice from beside her. Samantha started, audibly gasping and laying a hand to her racing heart as she turned.

"Where did you come from?" she asked Alexis, who was grinning like the cat who ate the canary. Mary stood beside her, a smirk on her face that said she shared Alexis's good humor—at Samantha's expense.

"Back door," Alexis replied with an off-handed wave. "Same as always."

That was the problem with back doors, Samantha decided. They could allow best friends to sneak up on her. There was no bell to announce them, although with the twitter they usually made, she was surprised she hadn't heard them coming.

"Did you ever think about knocking?" she groused.

Alexis hoisted one dark blond brow. "And why would we do that?"

She was right, of course, though Samantha was loath to admit it. There was no good reason for her friends to all of a sudden start knocking when they stopped by. They'd been visiting the shop unannounced since they were all in kindergarten together. This had to be the one and only time they hadn't made enough noise to be a circus parade—and of course it was when she'd really needed them to broadcast themselves.

This time, they'd come in on the sly and caught her staring at Will—which, of course, Alexis had announced in a none-too-quiet voice. It was unlikely that he hadn't heard her outburst.

"We've been here for a while now," Mary added. "We were eavesdropping on you and Will from the back room. That little girl Genevieve sure is a cutie. And Will is—" She broke off her statement with a sigh. "If you ask me, there's potential."

Samantha did *not* want to ask what kind of *potential* her dear friends had in mind.

"How is Sergeant Sweetheart working out for

you?" Alexis asked with a loud chuckle. "Have you set a date yet?"

Will glanced in their direction, his brown eyes flickering with surprise. Samantha knew the best part of valor in this instance would be retreat.

Quickly.

"Sidebar," Samantha hissed, shaking her head. She grabbed each of her friends by an elbow and propelled them into the back room. "He was a corporal. And would you mind *not* bringing attention to him?"

"He's handsome," Mary disputed. "And single. You're single. I don't see the problem with it."

"Okay, there are a lot of problems," Samantha said, "but let me just start with three. One, he isn't single—he's a widower. Quite recently, I might add. Two, he is shy. And three, he is here to build a relationship with his daughter, not to have a romantic tryst with me, or any other woman in Serendipity, for that matter."

"Strong and silent," Alexis said, stroking her chin thoughtfully.

"What?"

"Not shy. Strong and silent. That's more poetic."

"More romantic, you mean," Samantha corrected. "And I don't like the insinuation in your tone, thank you very much."

"Will lost his wife, but that doesn't mean he has to be alone forever," Mary protested. "He deserves someone special in his life. I'm not saying you're going to marry him tomorrow or anything, but you could at least give him a chance when he's ready to move on."

"What I'm giving him," Samantha explained, thoroughly exasperated with both of them, "is space. And that's what you two ought to be doing, too. He's still grieving. Leave the poor man alone." She knew as she said it that that wasn't likely to happen.

Her friends would keep pushing and she'd balk, just like always. Whenever she'd start dating, her friends would be quick to call for further commitment, but it never happened that way. She'd find some reason or other to break things off.

She didn't know why. As cliché as it might be, it wasn't the men, it was her. She believed marriage was God uniting two hearts in an inexplicable way. And until she found that, she saw no point in pursuing anything with anybody. Especially not with Will, who wasn't even a Christian.

"Samantha?" Will called from the front room.

"Can you give me a hand? I'm having a bit of trouble with the register."

It didn't surprise her that Will couldn't pick up on the rusty machine. The cash register was older than she was, the ancient iron punch-the-dollar-sign kind that had faded out with the advent of the first computer. It fit the country feel of the grocery, though, so Samantha had kept it. She'd been using it for so many years she didn't think twice about it, but she could definitely see where Will might get confused.

"I'm going back in there to serve my customers," Samantha whispered. "And you two are going to get out of here and leave us in peace. Please, *please* promise me that you won't put Will on the spot."

"Yes. No. Maybe so," Alexis responded with a matchmaking gleam in her eye.

"So what do you do for fun around here?" Will asked as he swept dust out the front door and across the clapboard sidewalk. Samantha had just turned the sign from Open to Closed and they were cleaning up before leaving for the night. "Ride horses?"

He thought it seemed like a reasonable question. So far he'd seen a lot of trucks on the road, and at least an equal number of horses on the ranchland he passed as he walked every morning from the Howells' bed-and-breakfast to the store, and then back again each evening.

Samantha stopped wiping the front window she'd just sprayed with glass cleaner and narrowed her eyes, one hand drifting to perch on her hip. "Why would you say that?"

"I don't know. I guess because I noticed the old hitching post in front of Cup o' Jo's Café when I passed it this morning. Watering trough, too, I think. The thing looks like it's been there for a hundred years."

Samantha shrugged. "It probably has been. Folks do occasionally use it when they stop at Cup o' Jo's, if they're out riding that way. It doesn't happen very often, though. We're not quite as backward here as you might imagine."

He held up his hands. "Innocent observation. No offense meant."

"None taken." Samantha laughed. The sound was unmistakably feminine and it mixed Will's insides all up. He cast around for something to say.

"Your friend Alexis reeked of horse when I met her." As soon as he said the words he realized how awful they sounded. He was used to saying what he thought without sifting it through the filter of what was appropriate in mixed company. Being around Samantha really messed with his head.

She lifted her chin, regarding him closely, the hint of a smile playing on her lips. He turned his gaze back to the cracked wooden clapboard and swept harder. It made him uncomfortable when she looked at him that way. Tingly all over, like last year when he'd caught a bad case of the flu and had suffered a raging fever of over a hundred and two degrees.

He remembered the incident well. It had already been inconceivably hot in Afghanistan, even without his fever. Every inch of his skin had felt like it was on fire, just as it did now. His breath came shallow and ragged, and his chest hurt with every lungful of air.

Not that being with Samantha was anything like catching the flu. It was a poor analogy, but it was the best he was able to do at the moment.

He couldn't pull the wool over his own eyes. He recognized the symptoms. The *honest* symptoms.

The bottom line was, Samantha was attractive in all the right ways.

"Sorry," he apologized gruffly. "My bad."

Again, Samantha chuckled. "No need. You're just saying it like it is. I don't think Alexis would be offended by your observation. She's a rancher and spends most of her time in the saddle."

"You're not easily affronted, are you?"

Her blue eyes locked onto him, and every

nerve ending in his body sparked to life. The emotions rushing through him engaged him in a way he couldn't even label. "Why would I be? If you can refrain from any more insults about women and erratic behavior, we're all good. Yes, No, Maybe So is more than a kid's game—it's a lady's prerogative. And don't you forget it."

Will chuckled. The woman was really something. She kept him on his toes. To his surprise, he found that he enjoyed working with her far more than he'd ever believed he would when Seth had first approached him with the idea.

But then again, he hadn't yet met Samantha.

"Why don't you see if you can find something to do in the back room while I tally the register?" she said, moving back to the counter and tucking the window spray and her rag underneath.

"Yes, ma'am," he answered, surprising himself with how upbeat he sounded. His heart felt lighter, too. Was he actually relaxing a little bit? Taking the edge off that gut-slicing sensation of guilt which usually burdened him?

As he entered the back room, his eyes scanned over the bins and boxes, looking for something to keep his hands and mind occupied.

There really wasn't much to do. Samantha kept her store in tip-top condition. Even her desk was spotless. Neither a paper nor a pen was misplaced.

He'd seen how hard she worked, even when she didn't have to. She was motivated by something beyond his comprehension, and everything she did, she did with a joyful heart. He'd never seen anything like it.

Will moved some of the boxes from the higher shelves onto the lower ones, making room for new product. Samantha was a tiny little pixie of a woman, five feet four at max. How had she possibly done all the heavy lifting all these years? Some of these boxes were heavier than she was, not to mention that the topmost shelves were completely out of her reach. The notion of her toting heavy boxes using only a footstool or ladder made his stomach twist in knots.

Whether she knew it or not, she would no longer be slinging heavy boxes around the back room. Not on his watch. He had just appointed himself Samantha's own personal muscle.

He scoffed at himself and shook his head.

He was here to do a job, which was the important thing. This was what he and Seth had talked about—how Will could fix Samantha's problems for her. That's all this was.

Will sorted through the inventory, organizing the boxes by category, rotating them according to date and lining them squarely over each other. He placed the older inventory within easy reach and shelved the newer products up top. It was only when he was nearly finished that he noticed that a small box of chewing-gum packages had been wedged in the far back corner against the wall. He'd missed it on his first go-round, and since the candy aisle was looking a little thin, he reached for it, thinking he'd stock the shelf with the extra bundles of gum.

He wasn't paying that much attention to what he was doing until he realized that moving the box forward revealed a file of papers wedged between the box and the wall. He couldn't conceive of how they'd gotten there. It was almost as if they'd been placed there on purpose.

Samantha must have been doing paperwork and had set the file down on the shelving unit, where it had been accidentally lodged behind the box and subsequently forgotten. It was probably nothing she couldn't live without, since obviously she wasn't tearing up the store looking for it, but he thought he should probably place it on her desk for her to deal with at her convenience.

As he set the box of gum aside, he bumped the folder and several papers fell to the ground. They were letters written on upscale paper, the fancy masthead declaring some prestigious law firm based out of New York: Bastion and Bunyan and Turner, Esquire.

The name sounded pretentious to Will, but then, he didn't care for lawyers. His only brush with them was after Haley had legally separated from him, and that had been bad news all around. In his opinion, lawyers tended to be seedy types more interested in making money than representing their clients with integrity and honesty.

But what did Samantha need with a bunch of New York lawyers?

Even with his curiosity piqued, Will had no intention of snooping, but his gaze unintentionally drifted over the first paragraph of the missive in his hands.

His breath hitched sharply as he realized what he was reading.

A threat against Sam's Grocery, written in particularly nasty legalese, on behalf of the giant corporation Stay-n-Shop. Apparently they wanted to buy out her store and replace it with one of theirs, as they had with other small groceries in the area. But they weren't asking—they were demanding. This was their third and final offer. And if she refused…

It was now a great deal more than curiosity that led him to flip through the rest of the correspondence. This was personal, engaging his warrior's heart.

These letters were menacing coercions from an adversary. And they'd been intentionally hidden. Will was sure of it. Anger stiffened his joints.

Maybe it was none of his business, but he was working for the Howells, for Samantha, and he couldn't imagine what they must be going through right now. Samantha must be frightened half out of her wits with this big corporation coming down on her the way it was.

What he *did* know for certain was that there was no way Samantha would allow herself to be coerced into selling. Not for any price. He hadn't been around the Howells for very long, but it was long enough for him to know they were a close-knit family in a close-knit community—and he'd heard dozens of stories about what life was like growing up in Serendipity from Seth.

Sam's Grocery was Samantha's legacy. She'd even been named after the store—or rather, *for* it. No *way* was Stay-n-Shop going to take it away from her. Inconceivable.

He didn't hear Samantha until she was right behind him.

"Hey, what kind of music do you like? We

can change the radio station if you want. I know country music isn't everyone's cup of tea."

Will instinctively drew the letters against his stomach, as if he could hide them from her. He shook his head. "Doesn't matter to me. I don't much care for music."

"How can a person not like music?" She sounded as astonished as if he'd just declared that he was originally from Pluto.

He shrugged. "I don't *dislike* it. It just doesn't matter to me one way or the other. Country, hip-hop, pop. Whatever. It's all the same to me."

"Okay," she responded, drawing out the word in a way that indicated she either didn't believe him or else thought he was off his rocker.

Or maybe both.

Will slowly turned around. "I rearranged your shelves," he said. Her eyes landed on the folder in his hands, and she blanched.

"You did *what?*"

"I pulled all of the older stock off the top shelves to make room to store the new product that will be coming in on Monday. I also rotated everything according to date." He held up the letters.

"And I found those letters Stay-n-Shop sent you."

For a moment, she just stared at them, wide-eyed and openmouthed. Her face went from white to green around the gills to a burning-torch red in a matter of seconds.

"Give me those," she snapped, snatching them from his fist and hiding them behind her back as if her action would somehow erase them from his memory. .

"Don't you think we ought to talk about it?" he prodded gently. He wanted to know what her strategy was so they could plan their next move. It didn't even occur to him that it wasn't his place to help her put this problem to rights. This was war—the more troops, the better.

"This is my *private business,*" she hissed. "Butt out."

Well, that was straightforward and to the point.

It was also wrong.

"I can help, if you'll let me," he offered, resisting the urge to reach out and touch her. The woman looked like she needed consoling and every instinct in him was screaming to do just that—and more. He suddenly pictured holding her close, wrapping his arms protectively around her, brushing his palm across the softness of her cheek.

His breath left his lungs in a rush, as if he'd been punched in the gut. He took a mental step backward. What was he thinking? He had no right to even consider acting out emotions he didn't understand himself. He couldn't—and wouldn't—hurt her as he'd done to others.

"I'm just sayin'. I work for you now—for Sam's Grocery. It's my livelihood, too, and I've got a daughter to look after. Clearly I have a vested interest in keeping this store alive and kicking."

Samantha gasped and then turned and fled the room. Will stared after her, astonished. He'd thought his explanation regarding his investment in her battle was unambiguous. Logical. Rational. So why had she run out that way? Hadn't she understood that he was saying he had her back in this fight?

Apparently not.

Chapter Four

Samantha bolted through the back door and into the country sunlight. Her chest was heaving and burning. She took big gulps of air, yet she felt as if no oxygen was reaching her lungs.

Will wanted to *help*, did he?

And for such laudable reasons, too. Not because he was concerned about her or her family, but because Sam's Grocery was his current place of employment. He was only worried about himself—but then, why wouldn't he be? He didn't know the Howells well enough to put himself out for them.

It wasn't like *he'd* have to worry about a job once Stay-n-Shop got their way and moved into town. Once they'd built their new store, Will would no doubt have his choice of any of a dozen positions, with his experience as a supply specialist in the Army. They'd be knocking down his door.

So what was *he* anxious about? *She* was the one who stood to lose everything she cared about, everything she'd worked for in this life— the intangible items that went far beyond the old clapboard building itself, like family, tradition, legacy.

And yes, she had to admit, that she was battling her pride and her deep-seated need to remain self-sufficient. She didn't like anyone in her business, especially someone she hardly knew. And yet the notion of sharing the worry that festered in her chest wouldn't let her go. The need to unburden herself was profound and powerful.

But if and when she shared her trials with someone, it most certainly wouldn't be Will Davenport.

And it wouldn't be her family. Not her father. Not her mom. Not Grandpa Sampson, who was known to spill a secret occasionally now that his mind was slowing down with age. It was out of the question. No matter how heavy a load she carried, it was vitally important that her parents not catch wind of her ongoing battle with Stay-n-Shop. She didn't want to mention it at all until they absolutely needed to know, and

Samantha desperately prayed it would never reach that point.

She wasn't ready to concede. Not yet. And in the meantime, what her parents didn't know wouldn't hurt them.

Her mom and dad, inheriting the shop from her grandfather, had struggled their whole lives for their family and the small-town community, working day in and day out to build Sam's Grocery into something stable and profitable. Only recently had they been able to pursue something different, to follow their own dreams and build their cozy little bed-and-breakfast.

There was no way Samantha was going to let Stay-n-Shop—or anyone else, for that matter—ruin that for them.

She didn't need Will Davenport's help. She didn't need anybody's help.

"Samantha?" Will said quietly behind her. He was close enough for her to feel the warmth of his breath on her neck. The man was seriously invading her personal space. She stiffened.

"What part of *butt out* do you not understand?" The guy had played all strong and silent, and he was good at that game. But now he was all up in her business? Why wouldn't he leave well enough alone?

"Look," he insisted, grasping her shoulders and turning her around to face him. "I know you're scared. And I'll back off if that's what you really want. But I can help you. I know I can."

"How?" she demanded. "How are you going to help me, huh? Do you have a law degree? Are you going to take on the corporate bigwigs? Rip up their letters? Fight them off with a stick?"

She knew she was being unreasonable, but so was he. Like he could just step in and make everything right. Sir Galahad riding in on his white horse with his lance and his sword, ready for battle, determined to save the day.

Wasn't going to happen.

"You can't solve my problems for me."

"You're right," he amended. He slid his palm from her shoulder to her elbow. "I can't solve your problem for you. But I can support you, and be there if you need me."

"What?" His statement caught her off guard—almost as much as her reaction to his touch. He'd barely traced a path down her arm, yet his fingers were warm. Reassuring and oh so real.

She was the first to admit that Will was an attractive man, but her reaction to the mere brush of his hand on her skin stunned her. She'd never felt this way in her life.

She needed to get out more.

"I'm your associate," Will continued.

Precisely. Reason number one thousand, four hundred and ninety-nine why I shouldn't be noticing the minty smell of his mouthwash and the well-toned muscles threading down his arms.

And most especially because, in essence, at least, they were arguing. She wasn't supposed to be *noticing* him at all.

It must be the anxiety she was experiencing, which she'd clearly misinterpreted as something entirely different.

That's what it was. She wasn't thinking straight.

"I hope you'll also consider me your friend." One side of his lip crooked up in a half smile. "I'll help you figure out what to do about this threat—if you'll let me."

"Thank you, but I don't need your assistance. I'm fine on my own."

"Are you?"

The sharp, confrontational tone in his voice made her bristle. Guess they really were quarrelling.

"Absolutely," she snapped. "And what makes you so certain I haven't already solved this?" The challenge in her voice was unmistakable.

"You don't sound too sure of yourself."

So much for unmistakable. Was her insecurity that obvious? She straightened her shoulders, determined to ride out this conversation on her terms.

"I know what you're going through," he continued, removing his hands from her elbows and jamming them into the front pockets of his blue jeans. His gaze altered, taking on a distant quality. She hadn't wanted him to touch her in the first place, but the sudden absence of his touch was as disquieting as the distant quality of his gaze.

"How could you know that?"

"Because I've been there." He took a deep breath through his nose and released it through his mouth. "I know what it's like to be overwhelmed by circumstances in your life. I've always been independent—probably too independent. More of a curse than a blessing. But there comes a time and place where you need to let other people in, you know? Allow them to help when they offer."

Samantha moved to a grassy knoll under a sturdy oak tree and dropped to the ground, sitting cross-legged on the cool lawn. Will followed, crouching next to her.

"I hear what you're saying," she admitted as her eyes met his. "But I have my reasons for keeping this to myself. It's a family thing, you know?"

"I respect that."

She expected him to say more. Instead, he held her gaze without speaking, his brows dipping low over the unreadable depths of his eyes.

"What?" she asked when the silence grew too much for her.

"You're stronger than you know."

She stared at him for a moment, figuratively openmouthed if not literally, and then she nodded, reluctantly accepting the compliment. Will was a rough-and-ready Army guy who'd been in active combat for his country. If anyone knew strong, he did.

"Me, not so much," he continued, his deep gaze shifting to somewhere over her right shoulder.

"How do you figure?" she asked. "You were career military until your wife passed away, right?"

He quirked his lips and nodded.

"Something noble and courageous compelled you to join the military." She held up her hand to stop his argument. Fleeing his childhood was hardly the most patriotic motivation for enlisting, but that didn't matter. Anyone who spent any length of time with him could see that he was Army through and through. "You re-upped at the end of your first tour, so serving your country was obviously important to you. And yet you gave up everything to take care of your little girl. That seems pretty brave to me."

He shook his head fiercely, denying her words. "I did what I had to do. You don't know the whole story."

He paused and scrubbed his scalp with his fingers. His expression was hard, his gaze haunted and bitter.

"I'd like to know more about you," she replied. She honestly wanted to know what made the silent ex-soldier tick. He had depths to him that she had yet to understand.

"No, you don't." He scoffed, turning his face away from her. As low and gruff as his voice had become, she barely heard the ending to his statement. "I'm not the man you think I am."

Will didn't know what had come over him. He had just blurted out a bunch of personal stuff he barely acknowledged himself, much less shared with another person. But there it was.

There *she* was.

Samantha.

Brave. Fierce.

Vulnerable.

His respect for her deepened to the point where—what? Unquestionably, he felt a deep desire to protect her, especially now that he knew the enemy she was single-handedly facing. The Howells must be feeling quite overwhelmed by now, Samantha most of all.

He desperately yearned for those qualities he knew he would never possess—certainly not the way Samantha did. Honesty and integrity came naturally to her.

She wrapped her arms around her knees and looked at him with a question in her eyes, no doubt waiting for an explanation for what he'd just blurted out.

Only he didn't know how to give it.

"I wasn't a very good husband," he admitted. Regret clogged his throat, making his voice low and raspy. "And I definitely wasn't a good father to Genevieve."

"How can you say that? I've seen the way you look at her, the way you interact with her. She's your world. And you are most definitely hers."

"It wasn't always that way. I was caught up in my job. I was away from my family when they needed me most." Will sat on the ground next to her, propping one elbow on his knee.

"How is that your fault? Being away from home a lot seems like a given in your profession. Was Haley unaware that you were going to join the Army when you married her?"

"She knew. She'd always known what I was going to do with my life. We dated in high school. She knew how much I wanted to get out."

He thought she might make him backtrack, given the open-ended statement he'd just made, but she didn't interrupt him. He was thankful. It was hard enough to dredge up these memories without bringing his father and his home life into it.

"Actually, I was already in the service when we married," he continued. "She believed she was ready to make the sacrifice and be an Army wife—at least, at first she did."

Their marriage had been a great deal more complicated than he was able to explain. But he took a deep breath and plunged forward. "I didn't give her the emotional support she needed to deal with life while I was away. As a result, she felt all alone and lonely, whether I was home or abroad. Even when I was stateside, my mind was on my next deployment."

Add to that my bouts with PTSD and it was the prescription for a rocky relationship. Who wants to sleep next to a man who wakes up screaming in the middle of the night in a full-body sweat?

He wouldn't have wished that on his enemy, much less the woman he had vowed to cherish until the day death parted them.

Will nearly groaned as he recalled the many knock-down, drag-out fights he and Haley had had. And how much silence had reigned between them when they weren't at each other's throats. "We grew apart over time, and became different people. It was awkward between us. I didn't deal with my issues very well. I closed myself off from her and wouldn't let her in, and in the end, it tore up my family. *I* tore up my family."

"What happened?" she asked. There was more than keen interest in her voice. There was compassion—and empathy.

Two emotions he absolutely did not deserve from her. From anyone. He warranted censure, not understanding. But something about her kindness compelled him to keep going.

"Halcy tried her best to reach out to me and be there for me. Far more, I am ashamed to admit, than I ever did for her. But at the end of the day, she couldn't handle the constant struggle and loneliness of military life. She had difficulties making friends, since we had to move around so much. But I think the hardest thing for her was her inability to continue her education. She wanted to be a child psychologist. Transferring from college to college was a nightmare."

He paused as the sharp ache of the past settled in his mind. "We'd been married for just over six years when she separated from me. Genevieve was maybe one year old at the time. She moved back to Amarillo, where her parents still live. We were both born and raised there. I think it felt safe for her to return to what she knew, and her folks helped her make a new life—without me in it.

"*Safe*. What a cruel joke that turned out to be." He closed his eyes and gritted his teeth against the pain clenching his gut. "My own daughter never really even knew me. Not until…" His sentence drifted off into a harsh silence.

It took him a moment to collect his thoughts. Samantha remained silent and pensive, simply watching him with compassion in her gaze.

"How did Haley die?" she gently prodded. When he did not continue, she backtracked. "I'm sorry. I'm being too pushy, aren't I? My curiosity often gets the best of me and I ask too many questions. Forgive me."

"No, it's okay. I started this conversation. I don't mind telling you."

Actually, he did mind. He minded dreadfully. If he had his way, he would never speak of it again. Never *think* of it again.

Yet he didn't blame Samantha for asking. He *had* directed the conversation down this path, although for the life of him he couldn't have explained why he had done so. Hers was a legitimate question, spoken with kindness. And he knew beyond a doubt that it was her kindness that would be his undoing.

He could handle judgment, but not compassion. This was his punishment, his burden to carry—keeping fresh his knowledge of the responsibility he bore for Haley's death, keeping it at the forefront of his mind for as long as he lived.

"She was killed in a gang-related incident." *Because of me,* he thought. "I'll never know all the details, beyond what the police were able to piece together. No one was ever charged or arrested for her murder."

Remorse settled heavily in his chest. Without saying a word, Samantha nodded, sympathetic tears in her eyes. It was almost too much for Will to bear, but somehow, it moved him to keep going.

"They surmise that it started as a mugging, given that her purse was found in a Dumpster and her wallet had been torn through. Her driver's license was still there, but the cash and credit cards were gone."

He twisted his lips as he recalled the details. "She was walking home one evening from her job as a waitress at a truck stop. A *waitress,*" he repeated, the word feeling like chalk on his tongue. She'd wanted to be—*should have been*—a child psychologist working in a fancy office in a good part of town, making more than enough money. But because of him, because she'd flown from their relationship, she'd had to pinch out a living for herself and their daughter any way she could. As a waitress in a truck stop. He hadn't wanted the separation in the first place. Even afterward, he'd wanted to support Haley and Genevieve, but Haley wouldn't take a penny from him. She'd wanted to be independent. Instead, she was dead.

He swallowed his gall. "She was stopped by a group of gang members. As best as the police can tell, when they tried to nab her purse, Haley fought back. And she was stabbed to death for her effort."

"Oh, Will," Samantha said. She reached for him, covering his hand with the smooth softness of hers and rubbing the pad of her thumb across his rough skin. "I'm so sorry."

"Thank you." She was incredibly gracious, especially considering he didn't deserve her sympathy. "What bothers me most is that they never caught the guys who did it."

He pulled away from her touch and got to his feet, stepping away so she wouldn't see him clenching and unclenching his fists. His blood boiled as he mentally counted to ten. He wanted to punch something, but he didn't want to show his anger and lack of control in front of Samantha.

"I have to live with that knowledge for the rest of my life. Had it not been for me, Haley would still be alive."

He had never before admitted that aloud to another human being. He felt like he was choking. He couldn't pull in more than a gasp of air no matter how hard he tried. For once in his life, he simply wanted to *breathe*.

Despite the slight relief that grazed his heart now that he'd finally opened up to the truth, he was mortified that he'd just blurted out his culpability to his new boss, of all people. She would have every right to fire him on the spot.

Even worse than that—what must she think of him now?

"You couldn't have known she was going to be attacked," Samantha protested. "You were a continent away, fighting in a war."

"Exactly."

His heart fell. She didn't get it. Frustration made his words a bit harsher than they otherwise would have been. "I wasn't there for Haley. I wasn't the man she needed me to be. If I had been, she never would have separated from me. She wouldn't have been in that dark alley in the first place. She should never have been walking home alone at night, especially in a bad part of town. If I had stepped up—if I had been a better husband to her…"

"That sounds like a lot of ifs to me."

"Yeah." He blew out a breath and leaned his shoulder against the rough bark of the tree trunk, staring unseeingly into the distance. She was a softhearted, benevolent woman. She wouldn't be able to see how he was at fault.

They remained silent for a moment, each with their own thoughts. Will was wrestling to contain the ugly guilt spreading through him, which always happened whenever he thought about Haley and relived the details of the terrible tragedy. He had no idea what Samantha was thinking, and he wasn't sure he wanted to know.

"We got sidetracked," he forced himself to say in a lighter tone. He should have steered this discussion back to her a long time ago. "If I'm not mistaken, we were talking about how you needed to learn how to accept help from other people."

"And I believe I told you that I didn't need any assistance."

He made a sound in his throat somewhere between a cough and a chuckle. The woman was nothing if not stubborn. She refused to let him help her and her family in this fight, but what she didn't know was that he was at least as stubborn as she was. He *would* help the Howells keep their store.

"And as *I* said, sometimes you need it. Pride can only take a person so far."

Samantha's gaze widened. "Is that what you think of me? That I'm prideful?"

"Of course not. I see the bigger picture." He crossed back to her. "Look. I know how hard it is to ask for help. But you do what you have to do. I had to depend on Haley's parents, who, despite their declining health, took care of Genevieve until I was able to be honorably discharged from the Army. I don't know what I would have done had they not been there to keep me on my feet." He gestured toward Samantha. "Once I arrived in Serendipity, you and your family stepped up to help a stranger in need. You've all shown me and Genevieve such great kindness. I can never repay you. But I do wish you'd allow me to try."

Samantha's cheeks shaded a deep, alluring rose. She scoffed. "I don't know how you could call my welcome to you a *kindness*. It was lukewarm at best, I'm ashamed to say. Not very Christ-like at all."

"Only because you didn't get a heads-up that I was coming," Will protested. He'd been around her enough to know she wasn't usually the type of person to see the bad side of a situation or a person. She was an idealist from her head to her toes. "You've already done so much for Genevieve. She can't stop talking about you. She thinks the earth revolves around Miss Samantha."

She chuckled and her face brightened. Will heaved a great sigh of relief. Maybe the world didn't *revolve* around Samantha, but it was definitely made better by her smile.

"I like her, too," she confirmed.

Samantha's blue eyes were shining with such sincerity and vibrancy that he was almost convinced there might be hope for his world. He didn't pretend to understand the depth of her gaze, but it affected him to the very core of his being.

A frisson of awareness skittered across every nerve ending in his body. He wondered if she felt it, too.

Never mind that. He pulled his mental brakes and put a tight grip on his response to her—the adrenaline that coursed through him and the way his heart was beating overtime whenever their gazes met. He supposed he could write it off as that of a man just coming back from a tour in Afghanistan, but he knew it was more than that.

Samantha was *special*.

But whatever was between them didn't matter. It *didn't* matter, because he wasn't going to let it. There was no way he was going to put himself in the position of caring for someone again. He was hazardous material and Samantha was too good a person for him to risk wounding her. Because no matter how hard he tried to prevent it, at the end of the day, that's exactly what would happen if he didn't stop this train before it started. The last thing he wanted to do was give her the wrong impression.

She had nothing to gain, and he had nothing to offer. End of subject.

He reached out a hand and helped her to her feet, careful not to touch her any more than was absolutely necessary; careful, in fact, not to stand too close to her, because he might run the risk of inhaling the sweet floral scent of her.

He didn't doubt that he possessed the strength of will to conquer those urges, if he put his mind to it, and he had enough respect for Samantha and her family not to toy with her when he had nothing of substance to offer.

He dropped her hand as soon as he was certain she had her balance and tunneled his fingers through his hair. He'd been a loner for most of his life. It shouldn't be difficult to maintain the facade of detachment.

So why was it that he had to continually remind himself that's what he needed to do?

"Are we finished?" he asked abruptly.

"Finished with work, or finished with our conversation?" She sounded confused, possibly a little hurt. He'd obviously wounded her by pulling back the way he had. He was sorry about that, but in the long run, she'd thank him.

"Both." He forced himself to meet her gaze straight on.

Her dark brows rose into high arches. She looked as if she was going to argue, and then apparently thought better of it. "Both it is, then."

She spun on her heels and started to walk toward the shop, but she suddenly halted and turned back. Her lips twitched as she narrowed her gaze on him, watching him carefully. He squared his shoulders and met her gaze.

"Will you be coming for Sunday supper? I know my parents really enjoyed having you over last week."

Up until that moment, Will had had every intention of spending Sunday afternoon with the Howells. Having not had much of a family life growing up, he appreciated the way Samuel and Amanda Howell drew him and Genevieve into their world. He almost felt as if they had become part of the Howells' extended family.

And the food was incredible. He'd never experienced anything close to the sizable country banquet they spread every Sabbath. He thought

Amanda must cook the entire week just to present the fixins she offered, extending from one end of their sideboard to the other.

But the way Samantha had asked the question, he had the distinct impression she didn't want him to come. He narrowed his eyes on her, but her gaze gave away nothing.

"Yeah, I'm coming," he said after an extended pause. "At least I was planning on it."

There. That should give her a clear way out—if she wanted to take it. She could tell him to make other plans, simple as that.

But she didn't. She just gave a clipped nod. "Well, fine, then. My parents will like that."

He had no doubt that her *parents* would like it. They longed for their son, Seth, to return safely from the war. His absence was especially felt at the dinner table, where his chair remained empty. Will didn't mind sitting in for him. And Samuel and Amanda adored Genevieve, treating her like the granddaughter they did not yet have.

"What about you?"

As much as he wanted to know the answer to that question, he hadn't realized he'd spoken aloud until he heard her abrupt intake of breath. He winced. If he hadn't previously hollowed out his own grave, he'd certainly managed to mine a wide chasm now. At the moment, burrowing into that foxhole and covering his head with his arms to protect himself from the fallout didn't sound like such a bad idea.

She raised a brow. "What *about* me?"

Will's throat worked as he searched for words, but he simply shook his head and remained silent.

Because *that* was a question he wasn't sure he wanted her to answer. Because no matter what she said, it meant trouble.

Chapter Five

Well, that was weird, Samantha thought as she laid out the Sunday dinner china on her mother's table.

Two days had gone by and Samantha still couldn't wrap her mind around everything that had happened during her conversation with Will. Yesterday she'd been thinking of confronting him, or at least picking up where they'd left off, but Saturday was always the most hectic day of the week for Sam's Grocery.

As if regular weekend grocery shoppers weren't enough to keep the store hopping, the traditional Fourth of July celebration on the town green was scheduled for the coming Tuesday and folks were planning their family picnics and loading up with extra supplies, so it had been exceptionally busy in the store. Though she and Will had spent the entire day together, they'd barely spoken, and even then only about impersonal subjects having to do with the shop. By the time the day was over, they'd both been exhausted and had parted without another word to each other.

But so far, Sunday had been a good day of worship. Samantha loved playing the organ for the service, and today had been no exception. It was her gift to the church and the congregation, and she was always happy to do it, no matter how crazy the day before had been, no matter how many problems continued to plague her. She set it all aside when it came time to offer up to the Lord the music she carried in her heart.

She was looking forward to spending the afternoon with her family, including Genevieve, who always brightened the dinner table with her sweet smiles and innocent chatter.

And, if she was being honest with herself, she wanted to see Will.

He'd said he would be there, and she knew him to be good on his word. If she could sit near him or pull him aside at some point, maybe she'd get a better handle on what had happened at the end of their conversation; although to be honest, she highly doubted it. The man was an enigma. Every time she thought she grasped what he was thinking, he turned the tables on her and went off in a different direction. Now that she'd spent more time with him, though, she was beginning to suspect it was a defense mechanism. She couldn't blame him for that—not after all he'd been through.

As soon as she'd arrived at her folks' house for Sunday dinner, her mother had put her to work laying out place settings for the meal, using their best tableware. It wasn't fancy china—not out here in the country—but it was Mom's best set, the one she used when guests were present at their table. She treated Will like a son and Genevieve like a granddaughter, but they were company just the same.

As she worked, Samantha turned over the conversation in her mind again, hesitating only for a moment when Will and Genevieve arrived and seated themselves at the table. She tried to avoid his gaze, but she couldn't help but glance at the man from time to time, nor could she help the way her heart leapt as she watched him amusing Genevieve by making animals with his fingers.

She knew the exact moment he'd shut down their conversation, the moment when she'd pushed him too far. Physically, he'd drawn away and his posture had straightened into rigid lines. His jaw had tightened until she'd been able to see the tendons straining in his neck. But most telling were his deep brown eyes, which had shaded over, fading to black. It was as if someone had dropped a dark curtain over his countenance.

She might have been distressed by his reaction had the man in question not been Will Davenport, but Will was a complicated man who often shut down when his emotions were tested.

What she found *odd* wasn't so much the fact that he'd pulled away from her but that he'd been willing to open up to her at all. Out of nowhere, he'd trusted her with sensitive information she hadn't even solicited, much less pushed him on. She knew he wasn't the kind of man to go all touchy-feely, which was just one more reason she was confused by his forthright admission.

She had to admit that it was courageous for him to speak on those difficult topics. It couldn't have been easy for him. Will was a restrained man, preferring to keep his thoughts and feelings to himself, and yet he'd shared a very personal episode of his life with her. She suspected that he didn't speak of Haley often. Her memory clearly pained him, and Samantha now knew that guilt and bitterness accompanied his tragic story.

Looking back at it now, it was easy for Samantha to see why Will had suddenly wanted to drop the sensitive subject.

The question was, where did they go from

here? She now knew his history. It changed the tenor of their friendship, as did his pushing her to allow him to support her against Stay-n-Shop.

He'd said what he'd said for a reason. She'd heard his message loud and clear.

He didn't believe she ought to face her war with Stay-n-Shop on her own. He wanted her to accept the assistance he offered.

But should she accept the assistance he offered? Could she let her guard down enough to allow him to stand beside her in this fight?

The idea— no longer fighting alone, having someone guarding her back—had its own appeal. Could she trust Will enough to let him in? To make him understand why she could not and would not share this burden with her parents? Would he keep her secrets?

With a perplexed sigh, she slid into a chair on the opposite side of the table from Will, Genevieve and Grandpa Sampson. All three were quietly eyeing the food her mother was placing on the sideboard. Samantha glanced at her father, who was sitting in his usual spot at the head of the table, his rectangular blue reading glasses perched on the tip of his nose as he completed the daily crossword puzzle in the local tricounty newspaper.

"Thank you again for inviting us, Mrs. Howell," Will said, nodding his head toward her mother. "It's an honor to share your table and be a part of your family dinner."

"It's Amanda," her mother corrected gently, a speculative look on her face. "Your folks weren't the family dinner type?"

Will shook his head. "No, ma'am. Can't say that we were. We usually ate off trays in front of the television, often in separate rooms. My pop wasn't home much during the evenings, and when he was—"

His sentence dropped abruptly.

Her mom approached Will's straight-backed figure and laid a motherly hand across his shoulder. "We can't help who we grew up with, son, but we can certainly make things better when we have families of our own." She shifted down the table to where Genevieve was sitting and leaned in to plant a kiss on the top of her head.

"Yes, ma'am," Will replied. "I'm hoping to do just that." He cleared his throat. "With Genevieve."

Samantha knew how very much he wanted that to be true. When he wasn't at work at the store or helping with her parents' B&B, Will spent all his time with Genevieve, learning what it meant to be a father. Anyone with eyes could see how important the sweet little girl was to him, and if the smile on her face was any indication, he was learning quickly and succeeding brilliantly.

Her mother reached for a pitcher of sweet tea and started pouring it into their glasses. "I was a foster child, tossed around from house to house in the Dallas area." Her gaze took on a far-off quality. "I had a good deal of trouble finding my way. Were it not for the Lord and Samantha's father, I don't know where I would be right now."

Samantha's jaw dropped. In the past, her mother had only shared pieces of the story with her, and she realized there was much she didn't know about her own kin. Unlike most of the other residents of Serendipity, her mother had been born and raised elsewhere. Samantha knew she'd aged out of the government system, but her mother had never spoken much of her childhood. Samantha was ashamed to realize she'd never given much thought to how her mother had grown up.

She'd never placed herself in Amanda Blake Howell's shoes.

How could she have been so insensitive, not to have known her mother had struggled through childhood? But then again, she'd never had a reason to suspect her mother had been anything less than happy. Amanda Howell was a cheerful woman, vibrantly in love with her husband of many years and clearly content with her family life. Her rock-solid Christian faith had helped many others in Serendipity make their way through adversity. However and wherever she'd grown up, she'd turned into a beautiful person.

"Thankfully," her mother continued softly, "for the most part, I was raised in good homes with churchgoing folks who cared enough to set me right with the Lord." She paused, an unfamiliar frown marring her brow. "But over the years it was inevitable, I suppose, that I'd stay in a few rough houses—I wouldn't go so far as to call them homes—where the money my guardians received from the government for supposedly keeping me fed and clothed didn't go to necessities."

She shook her head as if to clear her mind of the unpleasant memories, and then her smile returned to her face. "I seemed to have fallen off track here. All I meant to say, my dear man," she said, nodding at Will, "is that I not only sympathize, but empathize with where you're coming from."

Her mother moved to the head of the table, where she stood behind Samantha's father and rested her gentle hands on his arms. Her dad covered her mom's hands with his, sending a loving glance and an affectionate smile over his shoulder.

"When I met Samuel," her mother continued, "he was taking classes at a community college and I was working in the cafeteria, trying to save up for my first semester of school. He ordered a grilled-cheese sandwich with a dill pickle on the side. I took one look into his big blue eyes and I knew I was a goner for sure."

Samantha tried to swallow around the lump in her throat. Her parents had been married for thirty-five years and they still shared a special spark. It was a relationship to which Samantha could only aspire.

Maybe that was why she was so reticent to form a relationship of her own. She was waiting for the kind of love her parents shared. Only God could provide her such a soul mate. Having a husband was one of the deepest desires of her heart, but it had to be the right man at the right time. Until then, she had a business to run—or *save*, rather—and a family to enjoy.

She smiled at her parents' beaming happiness. No way was Samantha going to let anything screw that up for them.

With a contented sigh, her mother finally took a seat next to Samantha and they immediately joined hands to say grace.

As she bowed her head, Samantha's heart lay

heavy with her unspoken burden. Her father prayed a simple blessing over their food and their family. Samantha's petitions were not as trouble-free. She prayed for Will, for him to find peace from all the grief that haunted him and for him to be able to bond with his little girl. She prayed for Genevieve, who was still facing major upheaval as she settled into her new town and school. She desperately prayed that she would find patience and be able to seek the Lord's will in her life, especially for guidance and clear direction on how to deal with the situation with Stay-n-Shop. What *could* one small-town businesswoman do against a large, well-financed corporation? The situation seemed impossible, when looking at it from a human perspective.

All things are possible through Him who gives me strength.

The Scripture verse was one she'd memorized as a child. It silently entered her mind, filled her heart, and gave her new hope.

She might be one small person in the big scheme of things, but her God was mighty. With God's strength and power, she could fight Stay-n-Shop, and she would do so with every fiber of her being.

But what she wouldn't do was involve her family. As she watched her parents laughing and sharing conversation over supper, Samantha renewed her determination to win this war alone. Anyone could see how happy they were, finally being able to live out their dream without worrying about Sam's Grocery.

When her mother spoke of expanding her opportunities to serve others through their new bed-and-breakfast, her entire face lit up with joy. And Samantha knew how much her dad loved to tinker around with construction and plumbing. They'd be in paradise.

And Will? Will had his grief to work through and his daughter to get to know. He didn't need the added burden of worrying about a grocery store he'd only been employed at for a few weeks.

No—this was something Samantha needed to settle on her own.

After the main course of country-fried chicken with sides of homemade potato salad, baked beans, deviled eggs and a cheesy broccoli casserole that was her personal favorite, Samantha rose and helped her mother clear the dishes.

"Anyone for pie?" her mom asked.

Will groaned in anticipation and patted his lean stomach. "I wish I had known about the pie before I took that second helping of chicken. I'm stuffed."

"I'm sure you can find a little room left in

your belly for a slice of Phoebe Hawkins's cherry pie," her grandfather commented with a satisfied grunt. "She makes the best pies in all of Texas, maybe in the whole U.S. of A."

Will chuckled and held his hands up in concession. "Okay, you got me. I'm a sucker for cherries, and this Phoebe Hawkins of yours sounds like a diamond."

Will's words immediately had Samantha bristling like a porcupine and wanting to point out that Phoebe was happily married with two children.

What is that? Jealousy? Over a woman who bakes a good pie?

Just because Samantha couldn't cook to save her life didn't mean she had nothing unique to offer the world. She played the organ for church every Sunday, and she was a crack shot with a BB gun. She could pop tin cans off a log faster than a person could number them.

Baking pies, indeed.

And what did it matter, anyway? It wasn't as if she was trying to get Will's attention—especially not after what he'd shared with her on Friday afternoon. The man was nowhere near ready to move on. He needed time to heal. That was exactly why he'd moved to Serendipity. To find peace and to spend time with his daughter. Yet more reasons for her to release whatever crazy notions that were constantly niggling at the back of her mind.

Samantha passed out thick slices of pie, stuffed to the brim with fresh-picked cherries and smothered with large dollops of whipped cream. Though in general she watched her portions, she allowed herself a small piece, seeing as it was Sunday. Sundays were special occasions. Sundays were all about dessert.

"You like your work at the store?" Grandpa Sampson queried of Will.

"Yes, sir," he answered promptly, scooping another large bite of pie onto his fork and swallowing rapidly. Apparently good pie *might* be a deciding factor in his life, Samantha thought with a little smirk at her own private joke.

"So it's going well, then," her father added. He was clearly pleased that Will had segued into daily life in Serendipity.

"Yes, sir," Will said again, directing a nod at her father. "I like serving the local folks. It's all good, except for this Stay-n-Shop nonsense. It looks like they're making good on their threat to set up competition in the area. If you ask me, they're wasting their time."

"What?" Samantha's mother screeched over the clatter of forks hitting dessert plates.

All eyes were on Will—except for Samantha's. She took in panicked glances from the people she loved most in the world, watching as their peaceful existences tumbled into a pile of rubble akin to the Tower of Babel.

She wanted to scream. She wanted to crawl under her chair and cover her head with her hands. She wanted to pummel Will for opening his big mouth.

What had he been thinking? He had to have known this would upset them. She'd told him to leave it alone. Why would he blow her cover on purpose?

"I—I'm sorry," Will stuttered, looking from face to face with a bemused expression on his face. "I just assumed you all knew. The correspondence I read…" He cleared his throat. "The first letter was dated quite some time ago. Naturally, I thought—"

His speech came to an abrupt halt as Samantha's father stood and slammed his palms down on the table, causing the dishes to rattle with the force of his impact.

"Samantha!" he roared. "Do you care to explain yourself?"

Samantha's gaze dropped from her father's frosty stare. "I have been… There are… We received…"

How in the world was she going to explain her rationale to her family so they wouldn't be angry with her for keeping them out of the loop?

Everyone was frowning at her. Even the message in her grandfather's eyes was clear and distressing: *I'm so disappointed in you.*

A mixture of conflicting emotions went off like Roman candles in her chest. Anger. Fear. Shame. Desperation.

"I didn't want to burden you with this," she murmured in a choked voice. Tears flooded her eyes. She had the distressing tendency to cry when she got angry, and she was spouting steam right now.

Her gaze narrowed on Will. *Thank you very much.*

He frowned as if to say, *How was I supposed to know?*

The answer hit her like a two-by-four. He couldn't have known. Because she hadn't told him. She hadn't told him that she was keeping her family in the dark about the Stay-n-Shop. So he hadn't realized the fight was hers alone.

The truth was, the situation with Stay-n-Shop would have come to light eventually, Will or no Will. What had she expected? That her family would be grateful? That there would be no repercussions for keeping it a secret?

She wasn't fool enough to believe they wouldn't be upset, but if she'd already resolved the conflict, at least their distress would be short-lived. They would be proud of her for saving the day. Now she'd never hear the end of it. That she'd kept the secret out of the best intentions of her heart was no longer relevant. Not to her father, or her mother, or Grandpa Sampson, who'd owned and operated the store long before she was even born.

"Genevieve, dear," her mother finally said, "why don't you go see if you can find your little dolly Natalie to play with? I think I saw her in the toy box in the play room. Or there's a video game set up in the living room, if you'd rather play that."

Everyone at the table waited silently until the little girl was out of earshot, not wanting to upset her. But the moment she was gone, all eyes turned to Samantha.

"You didn't want to burden us with *what?*" her mother demanded in the clipped mom voice Samantha immediately recognized as censure.

Samantha cringed. She might be a full-grown adult, but her mother was still her mother. She sat back in her seat, wrapped her arms in front of her and stared at her untouched plate of pie. The cherries, which only moments before had appeared delicious and mouthwatering, now twisted her stomach. She knew she'd never be able to hold down a single bite.

She'd essentially been outed, and now she had to deal. When her family discovered the full extent of Stay-n-Shop's manipulation, and all that she was keeping from them, she might not be invited back for Sunday supper until she was ninety.

What was she supposed to say?

"Do you want me to take this?" Will asked when she didn't immediately offer an explanation.

She shrugged and glared at him for good measure. *He* was the reason she was in this position. He might as well be the one to finish the job. Her head was already on the chopping block, and he held the razor-sharp ax above her neck. All he had to do was swing it.

"Samantha has been receiving aggressive correspondence from Stay-n-Shop," Will confirmed, his mouth a hard line of disapproval. She wasn't certain whether his scowl was meant for her, because she'd kept this situation from her family, or for the dire circumstances in general.

"We're all aware that they've been buying up local grocery stores in the area," her grandfather said. "Are you sayin' they're wanting to do the same to us? Take us out and put up one of theirs?"

Will's gaze brushed over her as he nodded grimly. The room erupted as everyone expressed their outrage and disbelief, shouting over one another in order to be heard.

Confusion mounted until her father put his fingers to his lips and whistled shrilly. He raised one hand in the air to take control over the ruckus. Still murmuring their opinions, the members of her family reluctantly quieted down. Will sat rigidly, his expression neutral. Surely he wasn't entirely unaware that his words had caused all this commotion. Samantha's blood boiled.

At least the guy should feel *something* after yanking the rug out from under her world. He'd altered the Howell family dynamic, maybe permanently. He'd quite possibly destroyed her parents' trust in her. Didn't he care about how she must be feeling right now?

"So what you are saying is that Stay-n-Shop has made an offer to buy us out," her father said to Will.

"Repeatedly," Samantha replied, but no one seemed to be heeding her words. She might as well not have spoken.

"Yes, sir," Will affirmed. "They're offering for the store. But there's more."

"More?" Her mother's head snapped up, her voice a good octave higher than usual. "Like what?"

"I told them I wasn't interested in selling,"

Samantha inserted, seething with frustration that no one appeared to be paying attention to her. It was almost as if they were ignoring her as payback, which she was the first to admit she probably deserved. Still, she had something important to say, and she needed them to listen. She spoke louder, increasing her volume to exceed that of the other folks in the room. "Believe me when I say I firmly declined their offers."

"Offers?" her mother parroted. "Plural?"

"Then why are we having this conversation?" her father asked simultaneously.

Because Will opened his big mouth.

"Because Stay-n-Shop wouldn't take no for an answer," she clarified. "They've acquired a ninety-day option on some property on the south side of town. They indicated that they would prefer to buy us out rather than build a new store, since it would be less of a hassle for them not to have to get new permits and zoning, especially since we already own the land around the store. They plan to use the additional space to build their superstore. However, if I don't cave in to their demands, they're fully prepared to move forward with building their own store."

"Consequently driving us out of business," Will finished for her.

Samantha's eyebrows hit her hairline. There was that *us* again. Will spoke as if he were one of them, as if he had a vested interest in Sam's Grocery beyond just working there. She felt like reminding him that he'd only been employed for a few weeks, and that she had hired him under duress.

She wondered if any of the rest of the family noticed Will's inclusive wording—and what they thought if they did.

"You received repeated legal threats, and yet you didn't think this was something we should be aware of?" her father asked Samantha in a barely controlled voice. He glowered at her as only a father could do. She didn't recall ever having seen him as angry as he was right now. His face was flushed, but it was his rhythmic stroking of the white goatee at his chin that made Samantha quake in her boots. Hopefully at least a little of that fury was directed at Stay-n-Shop and not at her. Otherwise, she was in the worst imaginable trouble. She felt like she was four years old again, getting in trouble for coloring on the wall. Only these markers didn't wash off.

Samantha took a deep breath and mentally pulled herself together. She'd always known this moment would happen—she'd only hoped it would have been *after* the issue was resolved. She'd wanted to present this as a closed case, without having to worry them with unnecessary details. But she had to accept that it was what it was.

"I kept this quiet for your sake."

"How do you figure?" her father snapped, thumping the table with his fist.

Out of the corner of her eye, she thought she saw Will wince at the gesture. But it was Will—he didn't wince. Not at anything.

"Honestly? Initially, I didn't see a reason for you to get involved," she answered. "Granted, I was a little shaken up when I got their first letter, but I thought if I declined their offer, they would go away."

"You should have told us," her mother scolded.

Samantha nodded. "I planned to tell you when everything was settled. But then those corporate lawyers came back with a second offer—more money, more pressure. They indicated their intention of securing land in the area should I not agree to their terms."

"Seems to me the tension is running a little high in this room," Grandpa Sampson declared. "Let's remember we're all family here."

"Samantha has yet to explain herself," her father said.

"She was doin' what she thought was best." Grandpa Sampson silenced her father with a look that could singe the hair off a human being. "What's done is done."

"What do you suggest we do then?" After Grandpa Sampson's admonishment, her father seemed to have calmed down a bit, though a muscle still jerked in his jaw.

"I think the first order of business is to get our hands on those papers," Grandpa Sampson suggested. He was in top form tonight, his mind clear. "We all need to read the letters to get up to speed, get a better sense of what's happening. We can't support our Samantha if we don't know exactly what we're up against. You can get them for us right away, can't you, Samantha?"

"I'll get the file when we're done talking," Will offered. "If you all can watch Genevieve a bit longer."

"Much obliged," said her father.

"It's no problem," Will insisted. "I'm glad to do it—to assist you any way that I can."

Her father nodded briskly. He understood what Will was offering, and it wasn't just running to the store to retrieve a file. He was stepping up for the family, just as he'd said he would. She didn't know whether to be relieved or feel bulldozed by his insistence on meddling in her personal business—or rather, the family business.

"Before you leave, Will, we should pray about it," her mother added. "God knows the specifics better than we ever will, with the letters or without them."

"I still have questions, Samantha," her father said. "You have yet to explain why you thought it would be better to keep us in the dark about this whole situation rather than coming to us for help," he reminded her. "We've worked our whole lives in order to bring you the security of the grocery, a legacy you could continue, should you so choose."

"Exactly my point," Samantha said. "You *have* worked your whole lives to give me Sam's Grocery, and I appreciate it more than you'll ever know. It's become my life's dream. Most all of what I want to accomplish in life is tied up in that store."

"All the more reason for you to have brought us in on this," her father argued.

"Or all the more reason for me not to bring you in at all," Samantha countered. "You finally have the opportunity to do something *you've* always wanted to do—run the bed-and-breakfast. Now I've ruined it for you, and don't say I haven't."

"How do you figure?" her father demanded, sounding a little bit wounded by her declaration. "You haven't ruined anything. It's hardly your fault corporate America is nipping at your heels. What you're saying doesn't make any sense."

"I don't think she meant any harm by withholding information," Will offered. "She really had the best intentions in mind by not telling you."

Samantha glanced at Will, surprised by his support. Did he actually understand why she'd not shared the information with her parents?

She knew she'd hurt a lot of feelings, and she wasn't sure how to repair the mess she'd made. She continued her explanation, folding and refolding her napkin in perfect lines to give her hands something to do. "I knew exactly what you would do if I told you about the situation with Stay-n-Shop. You would have set aside your own plans in order to help me until this whole mess was resolved. I mean, that's what you're going to do, isn't it?"

"You'd better believe it," her mother agreed.

"Absolutely," her father said at the same time.

"But don't you see? I didn't want you to do that. I still don't."

"Why not?" Grandpa Sampson asked. "The Good Book says that in a multitude of counselors there is safety."

Samantha threw her hands up in surrender. How was she supposed to argue with the Bible?

"I'll admit I may have made a tactical error in not bringing this to you sooner. Maybe I do need help. I'm not having any issues keeping Sam's in the black, but we don't have enough savings to hire a lawyer—definitely not the kind of lawyer we'd need to fight an enormous corporation like Stay-n-Shop."

"Then we'll have to find another way to win this battle—without a lawyer," her father stated grimly, and Will nodded in agreement. "It's up to us to find a way to fight back on our own."

Samantha felt oddly comforted now that she had other people by her side to support her. Maybe Will had been right. At the very least, she felt a little less defeated now that her family was with her. Even in their anger, she felt their love.

"I'm beginning to think I know what David must have felt like facing off against big old Goliath with nothing more than a sling and a few stones," Samantha admitted.

Will chuckled.

Chuckled.

She wanted to hurl something at him. Like her napkin. Or a brick. He just *had* to rub it in.

"Now you all are aware that I've never been to Sunday school," he said wryly. "But if I'm not mistaken, didn't David win that battle? Seems to me it all worked out well for him in the end, having God on his side and all that."

"You're exactly right, young man," Grandpa Sampson agreed with a satisfied grunt, as if he'd thought of it himself. "The Good Book says that the Lord our God is with us, the Mighty Warrior who saves. We can rest on that promise."

"I just hope we can locate vulnerability in our giant," Samantha said. "We need to find a chink in Stay-n-Shop's armor. Otherwise, we won't be slaying it with a dozen stones."

Before she realized what he intended to do, Will reached across the table and grasped her hand. Samantha was cognizant of the way the various members of her family were now staring at her with open curiosity and some amusement. But even more than that, she was ultra-aware of the gentle graze of Will's hand on hers. It was electric.

Her mother grinned like the proverbial cat who'd eaten the canary.

"It'll happen," Will assured her in his rich, firm tone. "We're going to beat these guys. You'll see."

Samantha scoffed. "And how would you know that?"

"Easy. Because I've seen your faith. And the faith of your family," he added. "If God is going to help anybody here, it's not going to be some huge, impersonal entity. It's going to be you."

"But you don't believe in Christ, do you?" she felt obligated to point out.

"I honestly don't know what I believe," Will

admitted, shrugging one broad shoulder. "Being around you folks has challenged me to reevaluate. I'm still asking questions. I'm not sure. Not yet. But you are, and as far as I'm concerned, that's all I need to know."

Samantha was astounded, not only by Will's support, but by his revelation that the Lord was working on his heart. It suddenly occurred to her that maybe there was a higher purpose at work, something larger than just the fight between an enormous bear of a corporation and a tiny ant of a country store.

That *maybe* filled her heart with new hope.

"Sounds to me like this would be a good time to bow our heads in prayer," her father stated, breaking into her thoughts. The family murmured in agreement.

Will hadn't yet withdrawn his hand from hers. Their gazes met and he squeezed her fingers, one side of his mouth creeping upward.

It had taken a man of no faith to remind her of her own.

She was not alone in this fight.

She never had been.

Chapter Six

Samantha excused herself from the table just after Will. She wanted to make sure she caught him before he left for the store to retrieve the letters. She had a few things to say to him and wanted to speak to him before she lost all the steam she'd built up.

Should she be angry or relieved? She didn't know, but she was certainly eager to find out.

"Hey, Will." She caught up with him just after he'd exited the front door. "Wait up a moment. I have a question for you."

He turned to her with a frown. Nothing new there. Anyway, she was the one who had something to frown about.

But now that she was in front of him, she wasn't sure where to start.

He arched a brow. "I was under the distinct impression you never wanted to speak to me again. You wanted something?"

Yeah. An apology.

"An explanation would do, for starters."

Will dropped his gaze and shoved his hands into the front pockets of his jeans. "I guess I owe you that."

"You think?" She blurted the words out before she stopped to consider that they were a little harsh. "Sorry. I spoke in haste."

"You're not the one who should be apologizing here. I'm the one who spoke out of turn today."

"Perhaps. Why *did* you tell my family about Stay-n-Shop?"

"Why wouldn't I?" He looked up, his gaze challenging.

"Fair enough."

"I had no way of guessing you hadn't shared the information with your parents. I know now that it wasn't my story to tell."

"No," she said, her chest weighted. "It wasn't."

"I still think they have a right to know."

She swallowed her first defense. He was right, of course, which was probably what galled her most. "Be that as it may, I should have been the one to tell them."

"Yes, you should have." His gaze was compassionate rather than accusatory, which only made her feel worse.

"I'm worried about you, you know."

Her breath hitched in her throat. "Don't be. I can take care of myself."

"Why did I know that was what you were going to say?" He chuckled. "You're the most self-sufficient woman I've ever met. All I'm saying is, you don't always have to be. Your family loves you, and they want to be there for you. I want to support you, as well."

She could no longer hold his gaze. "Yes. Well, thank you for that."

He cleared his throat. "I guess I ought to get over to the store and get those papers. Your folks and your grandpa are waiting."

"Sure. Okay."

He nodded and walked away.

"Oh, Will," she called. "One more thing."

He turned back.

"I'm going over to the church to practice the organ for next week's services, and I was wondering if Genevieve could tag along. I thought she might enjoy playing around with the keys and hearing how a pipe organ sounded."

As the church organist, Samantha tried to spend at least a couple of hours practicing on the actual instrument—plus, there was something exciting about playing an instrument with that much power. She had an electric keyboard at home, and her parents owned a piano, but it wasn't the same as being surrounded by the glorious, melodic tones of the pipes.

Will hesitated for a moment. His lips twitched as if he were about to say no, but then he nodded. "I'm sure she would. How does a pipe organ sound, anyway?"

"Loud," she teased.

He was hovering, waiting for something. Samantha guessed he wanted an invitation to come along.

She hesitated. Perhaps she should invite him. It might be the right thing to do. But right or wrong, she needed space, time to process her thoughts and emotions.

"I'll have her back by five."

"All right, then." Once again he headed off toward the store. She watched until he turned the corner at the street's edge and she could see him no longer. Only then did she let out a long sigh.

She considered going back inside to spend a little time with her family before heading to the church, but she was still a little shaken up by the day's events, and she doubted anyone was going to let the Stay-n-Shop issue drop, which was all the more reason for her to make herself scarce. At least until Will came back with the letters and her parents and grandfather had time to read the corporate missives for themselves, pray over the situation, and allow their emotions to cool off a bit.

They might be angry now, but she knew that their prayers would allow them to come back to the figurative table with level heads. She didn't blame them for being incensed. Yes, they were Christians, but they were still human, and she knew she'd just disappointed them fiercely.

She made her way to the living room where she knew she'd find Genevieve, who was sitting cross-legged on the floor with a video-game controller on her lap. The television was playing and replaying a loop of music on the introductory screen of a preschool learning game. The TV was blaring a bit too loud for a song that was, in Samantha's opinion, obnoxious to begin with. Genevieve sat rocking herself in a soothing motion, staring blankly at the screen.

"Genevieve, honey, do you need help playing this game?" Samantha asked gently, sliding down on the floor next to the little girl and folding her legs in front of her.

Genevieve shook her head and continued to stare at the screen, her pink lips curling down at the corners.

"Do you want me to find a different game for you? I'm sure we have more choices around here somewhere."

Again, the little girl shook her head.

Samantha's heart sank as a realization hit her like a bullet to her chest, and made her stomach turn over in nauseating waves.

Genevieve had heard the grown-ups arguing in the other room.

The sweet girl was extra sensitive. Even if she hadn't understood the content, it wouldn't have been difficult for her to pick up on the tone.

Poor little thing. She'd been sitting here listening to the adults raising their voices at each other when they'd all assumed she was thoroughly engrossed in the playroom.

"Shall we turn off the TV and do something else?" Samantha suggested.

Genevieve nodded and turned her expressive brown eyes to Samantha. Samantha's breath caught. The little girl looked so very much like her father.

"Have you ever played a piano?"

Genevieve's gaze brightened but she shook her head. Sensing interest, Samantha had a gut feeling she was onto something. She'd noticed how intrinsically rhythmic the child was when playing with pans and spoons in the kitchen. And Genevieve often sang to herself when she thought no one was watching. Samantha suspected the little girl had a creative and artistic temperament—something with which Samantha was intimately familiar.

Music always brought Samantha peace. Maybe it would likewise benefit Genevieve.

"Well, we have a nice piano here at this house that you can play any time you want to, but at the church I've got an even better one. It's called an organ, and it makes all kinds of cool sounds. You can try it if you want."

"Yes, please." Genevieve's polite words were laced with excitement. It was touching how Will was teaching her manners.

Just one more way Will Davenport had reached Samantha's heart. How could she stay angry at a man who cared so much?

Will took a deep breath of country air. It was nice to be able to walk from the Howell's back to the cabin where he was staying, rather than having to drive everywhere as he'd had to do in Amarillo. Walking gave him time to consider all that had happened.

It was hard for Will to consider Samantha taking Genevieve somewhere without him, but he no longer felt the panic he'd experienced every time his little girl left his sight, as he had when he'd first come to Serendipity. Each day he found himself able to release her more, bit by bit, giving her the room she needed to grow into a healthy, confident child. He would have been apt to smother her to death had he not had

Samantha there to temper his efforts. With her assistance, he was finding it easier to let his daughter go.

Samantha, on the other hand, was a different story. With every day that passed, he found his thoughts lingering on her more and more—and he wasn't just trying to find a solution to her problems with Stay-n-Shop.

It was Samantha herself who had his head and his heart in a regular muddle—all beautiful, generous, five feet four inches of her. He admired how, for the legacy of Sam's Grocery, she bravely stood as a buffer between her family and the big-box store, and how she'd wanted to protect everyone from pain and heartache.

He'd put her into a tight spot when he'd accidentally blurted out information he'd mistakenly believed the Howells had already known, and yet he had no doubt that the family would quickly mend their differences and pull together as a team. Samantha might have gone about it in the wrong way, but her heart had definitely been in the right place, and her family knew it.

Even with all the drama and tension, the Howells supported each other. As far as Will was concerned, this would be the day that he remembered as the first time he'd ever really understood what family was all about.

The only time Will had ever experienced anything close to that kind of solidarity had been in the military, on the ground in Afghanistan. Out there, soldiers had to have each other's backs.

What was it like to experience that kind of love and unity in a family? He was hoping to create that for his daughter. Would that he could give Genevieve the kind of strength and reassurance the Howells shared, so that she never had to fear she was alone.

Samantha was a great help in that area, offering Genevieve a good deal of stability and a friendly hand to hold. She had quickly stepped up for the girl as someone Genevieve could admire and emulate. Will found he didn't mind if Samantha wanted to add the faith element to her time with Genevieve. He knew that Samantha's relationship with God was a vital part of what made her the strong, compassionate woman she was. How could he possibly want any less for Genevieve?

Churches weren't his thing, and playing an organ didn't sound all that great to him, but he suspected Genevieve was going to love it—and Samantha had somehow instinctively known that.

As he neared his cabin located on the river's edge, he realized that being alone didn't sound all that appealing to him. The cabin would seem awfully empty without Genevieve. She filled up the room with—

Life.

Love.

He'd seen a lot of sadness and death—more than he cared to remember. Genevieve put him in a better place. She belonged with him now, by his side, with her little hand in his large one. He wondered how he'd possibly gone four years without really knowing her and being the father she deserved.

First tooth. First word. First step.

He'd missed all of that. One more regret that he would have to live with for the rest of his life.

He paused and swallowed the emotion burning in his throat. He silently vowed not to miss any more of those moments. Maybe he would take a peek in at the church and see how Genevieve was doing.

He adjusted his stride and turned left on Main Street, heading toward the steepled white chapel near the edge of town. As he approached, he noticed a sign staked to the undeveloped property across the street, and realized with a start that *that* was where Stay-n-Shop was threatening to construct their store. How ironic that the giant corporation wanted to build on that particular piece of property.

Selflessness versus greed in two blinks of an eye.

Except Will wasn't going to let that happen. He would do whatever he had to do, but he wouldn't stand there and watch the Howells' legacy go down like a sinking ship.

As he turned his attention to the church, he noticed one of the welcoming red doors of the chapel was propped open, and even at a distance he could hear deep, soulful music that threaded its way inside him, drawing him nearer.

Will had never in his whole life had an emotional reaction to music. No matter what kind of tunes were playing, they had never touched him or moved him. For him, music had been nothing more than white noise in the background.

But now it was as if the music wound around and through him, increasing in strength with every step he took, tugging him nearer.

Samantha was at the keyboard. It was fairly obvious that his daughter was there, as well, if the occasional discordant notes were any indication. He was impressed by the way Samantha played on regardless of Genevieve's help, maybe even encouraging the little girl to continue. He listened as notes poured from the instrument, seamless and beautiful as she allowed his daughter to join in the experience.

Will stopped just short of the door, feeling

more awkward and reticent than ever before in his life. Marching into battle wasn't as challenging for him as walking into this church right now. Why was this so difficult for him? What was he afraid of?

Was he afraid he might discover he was wrong about God?

Church is for good people. The distant echo of his father's voice filled his mind as if he'd heard it yesterday. Will, as a youngster, watching his friends with their Bibles tucked under their arms as they made their way to Sunday school at the local chapel.

You can't go to church. You're not a good person.

This was ridiculous. It wasn't as if Jesus was going to walk up to him and charge him with all of his many failings. God's censure wouldn't be found within these four walls. God's sanctuary was far more than plaster and plywood. If Will had learned anything from his time with the Howells, it was that God was found within his people. That's who made the true difference. In his life. And in Genevieve's.

He stepped through the door and followed the sound of the organ to the sanctuary where the people of Serendipity worshipped. Deep oak-colored pews lined both sides of the room, with a wide, red-carpeted runner down the center. A large cross hung quite visibly up in the front, but his eye caught instead on a multicolored stained-glass window. The sun's bright rays were pouring through it, giving the picture of Jesus with his arms opened wide in welcome an ethereal quality that sent a frisson of awareness up Will's spine.

Unnerved, Will dropped his gaze to the white-linen-covered altar in the front. On the right wall were more pews—Will guessed for the choir—and on the left was the organ, from which came both melody and laughter.

Samantha slowed the pace of the music toward the end of the piece, finishing with a full, dramatic set of chords.

"Your daughter is quite the organ player," Samantha commented, peering around the side of the organ and waving him forward.

"I can hear that," he responded, starting in surprise. He didn't know how she could have possibly seen him enter when she was in the midst of playing what to Will sounded like a complicated piece of music. Her fingers had been flying over the keys in swift and complicated runs, up, down and then back up again. At the same time, without missing a beat, she was caring for his child—teaching her, even. The woman could definitely multitask.

"Come look," Samantha encouraged. "Genevieve knows how to find middle C."

He cracked a grin. "I assume that's an important skill in organ-hood," he quipped.

"You'd better believe it," she shot right back at him. "In piano-hood, too. The first step to a career as a concert pianist."

"That sounds good to me," he quipped.

"Daddy!" Genevieve exclaimed as he approached the organ, launching herself into Will's arms from where she'd been crouched next to Samantha on the bench. It was a good thing serving in the military had given him quick reflexes or he wouldn't have caught her. The little thing was as nimble as a chimpanzee, and every bit as quick.

Genevieve kissed his cheek and then wiped her mouth with the back of her hand.

"Yucky," she stated definitively.

Samantha chuckled, and Will joined in. "Are you trying to tell me that I taste bad?"

The little girl scowled adorably and shook her head. "No, Daddy. You have a scratchy face."

He ran a hand along his lightly stubbled jawline. He supposed he hadn't used a razor in a couple of days, maybe because he was no longer required to do so. "I guess I need to shave, then. What do you think, Miss Samantha?"

"Oh, I don't know," she said. "I kind of like

the unshaven look on you. It makes me think *manly* and *rugged.*"

Will decided right then and there that he was going to keep those whiskers. He felt as if he were glowing like a fluorescent bulb. He beamed at Samantha.

"All right, Monkey," he said to Genevieve, who was, in fact, swinging on his arm as if he were a jungle gym. "Why don't you crawl on over there by Miss Samantha and show me who or what a middle C is?"

Genevieve scrambled back onto the organ bench, scooting in close to Samantha. It was an intimate and trusting move that made Will's heart warm. He stepped behind the ladies so he could better observe the process.

"Do you remember what to do?" Samantha prompted, holding up her right hand with her fingers spread wide and gesturing toward the top set of keys, only faintly indicating where the little girl's fingers should go.

"Use my thumb and not my pointer," Genevieve recited from memory.

Impressive. Samantha had had his little girl here at the church for all of, what, half an hour? And already she'd taught Genevieve to differentiate between her thumb and her index finger.

Will was definitely impressed.

"Ready? Set? Play!" Samantha exclaimed.

Genevieve's thumb came down on the key at an angle, so there was a bit of discord at the beginning, but whatever key she'd landed on, she held onto it like a pro, the note echoing deeply through the pipes.

"Way cool, honey," Will praised enthusiastically, meeting Samantha's gaze over the top of the little girl's head. He raised his brow in an unspoken question. *Right note?*

Not that it would change how he was feeling right now. His heart was filled with so much love and delight that he thought he might burst from the mere pressure of the emotions. He was so incredibly proud of his little music aficionado that it didn't matter what note she played.

"Middle C," Samantha crowed in delight, beaming as bright as the sunshine streaming in the windows. "Way to go, Genevieve!"

If Will's little girl was going to become a concert pianist, he owed it all to Samantha.

"Way to go, Genevieve!" she repeated.

He nodded in agreement, and then amended the statement slightly in his mind.

Way to go, Samantha.

Chapter Seven

Will knew something was wrong the moment he heard Samantha gasp.

It was Thursday and the shop had been slow, so they'd decided to close up a little early. He'd been caught up listening to the twangy country song Samantha had been blasting from her radio as he swept the back room while Samantha counted down the till in the front, but her exclamation was audible enough for him to hear it even over the noise.

Or maybe he was just so in tune to her that he could *feel* her distress. Either way, his response was immediate.

Dropping his broom, he quickly emerged from the back room. Samantha's face was as white as a sheet. Her lips were tight and her pulse was pounding at the base of her neck.

He moved to her side, ready to suggest she

pull up a chair and sit down to get her bearings when he saw the visitor standing just inside the front door. He was a tall, rangy man in a designer, pin-striped blue suit, complete with an elegantly folded white handkerchief protruding from the coat pocket and a camel-colored leather briefcase. He had a long nose and slicked-back black hair that put Will in mind of a vulture. He was one of those guys women might consider exceptionally good-looking—and he knew it. And knew how to use it, if the syrupy smile he flashed Samantha was any indication. The man reeked of overinflated ego and money.

To Will's relief, Samantha appeared to be having none of it. Her expression hardened and she tipped her chin resolutely. She looked ready to do battle. Will shifted behind her right shoulder, subtly reminding her that he had her back.

If the situation hadn't been so serious, Will would almost have felt sorry for the stranger. *Almost.* He'd been on the receiving end of Samantha's glare more than once, and he knew how uncomfortable it was, but it didn't appear to bother the spiffed-up, slicked-back fellow who still wore a confident, borderline-arrogant grin.

The guy set the hair on Will's neck on end. He was polite, charming even, but something about the situation struck Will as off.

Perhaps there was no reason to worry. It was possible that Will was misreading Samantha's signals. The blush now prettily staining her cheeks could just as well be from delight and not from distress.

But Will was a man who had long ago learned to go with his gut. His instincts had saved his hide countless times in the military. And right now every nerve in his body was screaming that they were in the midst of a minefield and he needed to protect Samantha.

Not that he had any doubt Samantha could hold her own. But it was with good reason that he'd been contending all along that a team was stronger than an individual. What was it her Grandpa Sampson had said? Something about safety in multitudes? Well, he might not be a multitude, but two was better than one. He'd learned that through his military experience and his family—and now, through the Howells. He owed them this, to be there for Samantha.

Besides, Will wouldn't be taken in by the man's easy charm or flattering looks.

The stranger laid a blue-backed document on the counter in front of Samantha and slid it her direction with the tips of his well-manicured fingers.

"My name is Cal Turner," he said with an unnaturally white-toothed grin and a hint of an

English accent. "I'm here today representing the interests of Stay-n-Shop."

"I know who you are," Samantha replied, smiling politely, although Will thought—hoped—it didn't reach her eyes. "And I know who you work for. What I don't know is why you are here. I've already said my piece and it appears you don't care to hear what I have to say."

"I'm sorry?" the lawyer queried. Clearly he wasn't used to being countered. Will suspected that Cal had thought that a small-town country store owner would be easy pickings, especially a woman.

His sweet talk wouldn't work on Samantha. She was too smart for that, and Will was positive she wouldn't take it lying down. This was going to be interesting.

"Look, there's no sense running around the issues here, so let's just be blunt," Samantha countered, her voice soft but firm. "It is my understanding that you've purchased a ninety-day option on a piece of property south of town. According to your new plans, you no longer need Sam's Grocery. And even if you did, I've repeatedly declined your offers, generous as they've been. How dare you approach me again?"

Was that sarcasm? From the astonishment written in Cal's expression, the lawyer certainly thought so. Her declaration was bold and brash and completely Samantha. Call a spade a spade and force the charismatic lawyer's hand. Will's chest swelled with emotion—pride, satisfaction and an enormous sense of gratification when the slick fellow's jaw dropped. She'd clearly caught him completely off guard, which Will expected was exactly what she was trying to do in order to give herself time to think her way out of the situation. Will was happy she'd seen through Cal's manipulative tactics.

It wasn't, however, perhaps the best course of action when it came to Cal Turner. Will knew plenty of men like him—eager to do anything for the right price. He wouldn't mind bending a few rules, or ignoring them altogether, in order to get the end result he desired.

At the same time, Will understood Samantha's anger—shared it, even. And she was right. This guy was here for a reason, not a social call. If Stay-n-Shop had already settled on building a store in Serendipity, they no longer needed her or her grocery. She was, in fact, their direct competition. So why had the man presented himself here today, with legal documents to boot?

Was it possible that the Howells' prayers had already been answered? Was Stay-n-Shop pulling out of the picture?

Cal's smile disappeared and his blue eyes grew dark. He tapped his fingers against the document. "This is your lucky day. I've been authorized by Stay-n-Shop to give you one last opportunity to sign a deal with us."

"And why would I do that?"

"You might want to look over this contract before you make any decisions," he advised brusquely. "You should be grateful and know a good deal when you see one. Stay-n-Shop has upped the ante for you, although in all honesty, I can't imagine why." He took a sweeping glance around the store, a disdainful expression on his face. Clearly the country ambience that was Sam's Grocery did not appeal to Cal Turner. So much for pleasantness and charm.

Samantha sniffed. She'd seen Cal's expression, as well.

"They're offering you more than they've offered to any of the other grocers in the area. What are you waiting for?" Cal offered Samantha a black pen that was probably worth more than Will had made in a month in the Army.

"Apparently you are hard of hearing," Samantha said in a scathing tone. "I have no intention of signing your document. It's never going to happen. So why don't you just turn yourself right around and go out the way you came in. I'm sure I don't have to show you the door."

"I suggest you think before you speak, young lady," Cal snapped, looking down his nose at her. Now there was no question that he was a vulture. "Are there any lawyers in this boondock town? Because I highly recommend you get legal counsel before turning down this offer—not that I expect any lawyers around here will be knowledgeable enough to assist you in this."

Samantha merely raised an eyebrow and pointed toward the door.

"You obviously don't know what you're doing." His once-smooth voice sounded strained. "You're opposing perfectly good terms for a store that isn't worth half what they're offering. You'd be able to buy a house." He waved a hand in an encompassing movement. "And what do you think all the people in your little town will think about this? Your store is nothing compared to what Stay-n-Shop can offer the people of Serendipity. Variety. Discounts. *Jobs.* If they decide to build, you'll be out of business within a year, maybe sooner. Mark my word on that."

"Is that a threat?" Samantha asked through gritted teeth, and Will slid a hand around her waist, curling his thumb through one of the belt loops on her jeans. She looked like she was about to spring at Cal like a rabid dog. Not that the guy didn't deserve it, but choking the life out of him wouldn't further Samantha's cause. In fact, it might make things worse. Otherwise, Samantha would have had to wait in line behind Will.

"Take my words any way you wish," Cal hissed. "This proposal has a time limit on it, and the corporation is unlikely to put such terms on the table again. In fact, I can pretty much guarantee you that this is the last opportunity you're going to get. If I were you, I would take it and run, before you have nothing to run with."

"Stay-n-Shop can build as big a shopping center as they want to. They can never offer the kind of personal customer service Sam's Grocery does. I know the names of virtually everyone who walks in my door. I have loyal customers who will never desert me. And if you think they will, you don't know the first thing about family legacies and small-town dynamics."

"Perhaps not, but I do know discounts. And I know how fickle people are once they've had a taste of variety. And you'd be surprised how quickly your *loyal customers* will switch to Stay-n-Shop once they realize how much they can save there."

Will could feel the tension in Samantha's back and knew how much it cost her to remain in control, yet she showed no signs of weakness.

Her shoulders were squarely set in determination and her gaze never faltered from the lawyer's arrogant glower.

Will admired her strength, but he had seen and heard enough from this slick Cal fellow. He shifted so he was standing just behind Samantha's left shoulder and slid his arm from her waist to her shoulders, grasping her firmly, keeping her steady as he reached across the counter with his other arm. Leveling the lawyer with a glare, he planted his palm over the contract and pushed it back toward Cal.

"I believe the lady said she wasn't interested," he said. "I highly suggest you take your legal mumbo jumbo and get out of here."

Samantha shifted her weight so that her shoulders rested against his chest. He tightened his hold on her even more.

"This isn't the last you'll see of me," Cal warned, swiping up the contract and furiously waving it in their direction. "Next time I won't be so nice."

"You'd better hope there *is* no next time, buddy," Will warned. "You should stay away from here if you know what's good for you." If this charismatic scavenger thought he could mess with Samantha, he had another thing coming. Like Will's fist.

Cal's gaze faltered just for a moment as his

eyes met Will's, and Will pressed his advantage, pointing toward the door. "I said go. Now."

Cal's gaze narrowed. "You can count on there being *a next time*. We're already in the process of scheduling a town council meeting, so this is *not* the last you'll see of me," he growled. Then he spun on his heel and fled.

When the man was finally out of sight, Will realized how tightly he was grasping Samantha and loosened his hold on her. A little.

Enemy thwarted. Crisis averted.

For now.

The moment Cal Turner was gone, Samantha melted into the strength of Will's arms. She'd been holding herself so rigidly that when she took a deep breath, her head began to spin and she saw black spots before her eyes.

She had no doubt that Cal Turner would make good on his threat. He'd be back—no doubt with a legion of corporate lawyers trying to press for what they wanted. It didn't help to know they usually got exactly what they wanted.

She wished they would just leave her alone.

But what if they didn't come back? What if this was, in fact, Stay-n-Shop's last attempt to buy out Sam's Grocery? Perhaps they would simply begin construction on their own site, in which case leaving her alone was probably not for the better.

She sent up a silent prayer of thanks that Will had been there with her and had her back, both literally and figuratively, during the crisis moment. She supposed she should feel humiliated and embarrassed that he had witnessed the scene with Cal's counterfeit fawning and flattery, but she only felt gratitude toward him. She wasn't positive Cal would have left without Will's physical bulk backing her up.

Literally backing her up. She had to admit, sometimes muscle was a good thing. His broad chest had been—still was, in fact—a haven for her. She'd drawn strength from the silent power of his intensity, making it possible for her to stand up to Cal and appear strong on the outside when on the inside she was shaking.

Now that the misleadingly charming, intimidating lawyer had left and the immediate threat was gone, she was quivering with an intensity that frightened her. Even her teeth were chattering. She swiped a hand over her face, trying to steady herself.

Will tightened his hands on her shoulders and turned her around, staring intently down at her face. His gaze clouded with worry. He led her to a nearby chair, urging her to sit. "Can I get you something? A glass of water, maybe?"

"No. I'm fine," she insisted, although she felt anything but *fine*. She set her jaw, wrestling to contain her emotions.

"Just try to breathe," Will murmured, crouching before her and meeting her gaze with his intense brown eyes.

"I am breathing." She hiccupped.

"Yeah, you are," he agreed with a wry chuckle. "Breathing *fire*."

She laughed despite herself, and he grinned back at her.

"I just want to make sure you're okay."

"I'm okay, mostly thanks to you. You really helped me out today."

"You did a great job all on your own." Will nodded and reached for her hand, stroking it lightly with the pad of his thumb. "But I was glad to be there for you."

For her. Did he really mean that, or was it a slip of the tongue?

It wasn't as if she could ask him, but when his grip tightened on her hand and his gaze turned dark, words simply weren't necessary.

Leaning forward on one knee, he framed her face in his hands. They were large, rough hands—the hands of a soldier.

The hands of her hero, at least for today.

One side of his mouth curled into a half smile. His face was close enough for their breath to mingle, and yet he made no move to kiss her. He just drank her in with his eyes.

"You can always call on me," he assured her, running a finger down her forehead, over her nose and then brushing it backward across her chin. "Day or night, whatever you need. I'm here for you."

She struggled with the desire to reach forward, grab his collar and finish what he'd started. But when he rocked back on his heels, the moment was broken. For whatever reason, Will had pulled away. She didn't understand it, but she had to respect it.

Even if what she really wanted to do was fall into his arms.

Chapter Eight

"How's our handsome soldier boy?" Alexis asked Samantha as they stood in line waiting to buy sparklers and cones that sprayed fountains of sparks. The church youth group sponsored the booth on the community green, where the traditional Fourth of July picnic and fireworks display would be held later that evening.

"You haven't asked us to be bridesmaids yet. What are we to think?" Mary gave Samantha a friendly nudge with her elbow. "You couldn't possibly have imagined that we were going to forget about him, now did you?"

"I could only hope," Samantha murmured sarcastically, handing the vendor a twenty-dollar bill for the sack of sparklers and fountains she was purchasing. She glanced across the green, where Will was busy setting up lawn chairs for her parents and grandfather and spreading a red-plaid blanket for the rest of their group. He swung Genevieve around in a circle and plunked her down in the middle of the wool blanket, chuckling as she squealed with laughter.

"You could only hope what? That you'd have a ring on your finger, or that we'd leave you alone?" Mary teased.

"Really?" Samantha rolled her eyes.

"Can we help it if we want to see our best friend settled down and living happily ever after?" Alexis gently prodded Samantha's ribs with her elbow.

"I don't know why you two are picking on me all of a sudden," Samantha grumbled. "I don't see either one of you showing off your diamond solitaires."

"That would be because our knights in army-green camouflage haven't yet ridden into our lives," Mary said with a sigh. "You are so blessed and you don't recognize what you have when it's right before your eyes. God just dropped him right into your lap."

Samantha snorted and shook her head. "I don't even know what that means. And trust me when I say that I don't even *want* to know."

"You can fool the rest of the world, but don't try to play ignorant with us. We understand you all too well. And even if we weren't besties, anyone with eyes can see the way he looks at you when he thinks nobody is watching him." Alexis's sly smile grew to epic proportions and her blue eyes sparkled with mischief. "Like right now, for instance."

"What?" Despite all her good intentions, Samantha turned to look at Will. He was seated on the blanket next to Genevieve, propped on one elbow with his legs stretched out before him, laughing at something her mother was saying to him. "He's not—"

"Ha! Made ya look," Alexis crowed. "Anyway, he *was* looking at you a second ago."

"That was so not nice," Samantha admonished, her face warming, but she chuckled just the same. She should have known better than to fall for that old trick.

Her best friends could always tell when she was down, and surely they'd noticed something was bothering her lately. She wasn't spending as much time with Alexis and Mary as she usually did. At first they might attribute her absence to her spending extra time with Will, but it wouldn't be long before they figured out there was more going on. She hadn't yet shared with them the trials she was facing with Stay-n-Shop, but it was only a matter of time before they picked up on it—and before the entire *town* knew what the large corporation had planned.

Alexis bought her own sack full of fireworks and looped her arm through Samantha's. "Seriously, now. No progress to report to us girls?"

"I guess it would depend on what you mean by progress," Samantha countered, seeing a way to lead her erstwhile friends away from their floundering matchmaking efforts. It wouldn't take them long to figure out they were on a deliberate detour, but at least it would take the heat off Samantha, if only for a moment so she could catch her breath.

"Will is doing well at the store. Far better, actually, than I anticipated he would." Despite her best efforts, her gaze kept drifting to Will, which she knew was not lost on her friends. "He actually seems to like his work, although he's a bit of a perfectionist. He takes it seriously, in any case, and puts a great deal of effort into whatever he does."

"Was there ever a doubt?" Mary teased.

"In my mind, at least," Samantha admitted. "He's fresh from Afghanistan. He's got to be used to power and adrenaline on a daily basis. I thought he'd be bored to tears in a minute."

"Maybe the peace and quiet is just what he needs," Alexis suggested.

"Perhaps," Samantha agreed, watching Will from under her lashes. As long as he didn't look her way, she was good.

"And he's a daddy. He has a duty before the Lord to be responsible," Mary added. "That means he *has* to be all grown-up and manly and everything."

Alexis let out a low whistle. "He certainly has the manly thing going in spades."

Samantha rolled her eyes. "You guys are too much. Just leave the poor guy alone. He's my employee, for crying out loud."

"Is that *all* he is to you?" Alexis asked merrily, her blue eyes gleaming with gratification. Clearly she believed she already knew the answer to her question.

Samantha broke her gaze away from her friend's torment rather than answering the question. It might be friendly fire, but it still put her in a dangerous position.

"I thought not." Alexis's voice dropped as she pulled Samantha to a halt underneath a large, stately oak, out of hearing distance of all except Mary, who was a step behind them. "So what is the deal, really?"

Samantha sighed. It was so much easier on her when her friends weren't being serious. When they were just playing around with her, she could pretend all was right with her world. Maybe it was just a subconscious thing, but sometimes when she was laughing with her best friends, she found herself able to cling to the past, remembering her high-school days when the most taxing thing she had to worry about was whether or not her hair was working and who was going to take her to prom.

But when Alexis and Mary started asking genuine, compassionate questions—hard questions—her emotions became engaged, and she found herself very much on the verge of tears—like right now. Too much stress, she supposed, from every angle. Enough to throw any woman, even a strong one, for a loop.

But she was determined not to break down in the middle of a community event. Especially not in front of her friends—she knew them well enough to know they would worry about her incessantly and make a big deal over her problems, which was exactly what she didn't want to happen. It was more or less the same reason she hadn't brought her parents into the Stay-n-Shop fiasco.

Alexis and Mary had her well-being and best interests at heart. They were far more than mischievous matchmakers—they were the closest friends she had. They loved her, and at the end of the day, no matter how much they teased her and gave her a hard time, she loved them right back.

"How do you feel about Will?" Mary asked softly, so her voice wouldn't carry.

"I don't know," she replied, knowing they would never break a confidence. "I'm attracted to Will, obviously," she continued. She didn't need the guidance of her two friends to tell her that Will Davenport was a treat to the female eye.

"And?" Alexis prompted.

"And nothing. There's really nothing left for me to say. You want me to admit I have feelings for Will? Yeah. I do. There's definitely chemistry where he and I are concerned. I just don't know what to do with it. I'm not sure I *should* do anything with it."

That was a gross understatement, she realized, thinking back to their near kiss just days before. She had needed his strength, and he had given it to her. She didn't harbor any misconceptions that there was more to it than that. It was the kind of special moment she'd waited her whole life to experience, but of course it had faded out as fast as it had appeared.

Will had backed away. And why wouldn't he? He was a principled man with honorable intentions, and he'd made those quite clear to her from the outset. She was just glad he'd been there when he had and that he'd had her back against Cal Turner.

"You guys definitely have sparks flying between you," Mary said, and then cocked her head and narrowed her gaze on Samantha. "Why do I feel like there's a *but* coming here?"

"Because there is," Samantha answered simply, riffling through the contents of the bag of fireworks she'd purchased so she didn't have to meet her friends' eyes. "Chemistry does not a relationship make."

"But you've got to admit it is a great start," Alexis said.

"In this case, no," Samantha denied.

"Why not?" Alexis was clearly not going to drop the subject, and even if she had, Samantha knew Mary would just pick it up again. Maybe it was better for everyone if she just set them straight on what was or, in this particular instance, was not happening between her and Will. Once and for all, and good riddance to the issue.

"Let me count the ways," she quipped, preparing to tick her reasons off on her fingertips.

"Can't wait to hear this excuse," Alexis muttered.

Samantha raised an eyebrow. "Do you want to hear this or don't you?"

"Of course we do," Mary assured her.

"All right, then. First, he's still grieving for his wife. He only lost Haley a few months ago." *Tick. Grieving* wasn't exactly the right word for what Will was doing—it was more like he was torturing himself—but the term would have to do for now. And it wasn't the whole story, but Will hadn't authorized her to share what he'd told her in confidence about his separation from his wife. He was a private man who played it close to the vest, and she respected that about him.

"We know all this," Mary confirmed. "Next you're going to say he's busy building his relationship with Genevieve."

"Well, he is," Samantha murmured, wondering why she sounded so defensive. *Tick* anyway, even if Mary had been the one to make the point.

"Of course he is," Alexis agreed. "Because he's a good man and a good daddy. Look at him over there playing a card game with his daughter." She gestured at Will, who was engaged in a rousing game of slapjack with Genevieve. "It seems to me that you're helping him out with Genevieve. The way I see it, spending time with Will and Genevieve should bring you all closer together, and it ought to be winning you a lot of brownie points, too, shouldn't it?"

"Not in the way you mean."

"Again," Alexis continued, sounding a little put out, "I probably shouldn't, but I have to ask—why not?"

"I don't think he's ready to commit to a new relationship."

"Because of his wife and little girl. Yada yada," Alexis said. "What is it you're not telling us?"

Truthfully, Haley and Genevieve weren't the reasons she'd had in mind at all, as valid as those points might be. Samantha was actually musing over what Will had said about his relationship with Haley *before* things had gone south with them. He'd openly admitted that he hadn't known how to be a good husband to his wife. Instead he'd pushed her away. Samantha knew him well enough to know that he generally tended to judge himself too harshly, but that didn't mean she didn't have concerns about his ability to dedicate himself to a serious relationship with a woman. And even if he was, who was to say *she* was ready? Perhaps her standards were high. Mary and Alexis both thought they were. And maybe they were right.

"He's not a Christian." The most serious *tick* of all. When the time came to walk down the aisle, Samantha was committed to tying the knot with another believer. Yoking herself unequally was a burden she did not wish to bear. She couldn't even imagine living a lifetime with a husband with whom she wasn't able to share her spiritual life. Her relationship with the Lord was far too much a part of who she was to dismiss it, even for the love of a man.

"He's not a Christian?" That stopped Alexis in her tracks and took the wind out of her sails, at least momentarily. "Wait a minute now. I'm sure I saw him in church last Sunday. Weren't he and Genevieve sitting with your parents?"

"Yes, that's right, but believe it or not, he told me that was the first time he's seen the inside of a church. Ever."

"Not even when he was a kid?" Mary asked, her curiosity piqued.

"Is he a member of some other religion?" Alexis queried simultaneously.

"No and no," Samantha replied. "My understanding is that Will didn't have the best family life growing up. I believe his father was a hard man, possibly an alcoholic, possibly abusive. They weren't a religious family of any persuasion."

"That's too bad." Mary's voice had softened and turned quite solemn. "Maybe the Lord will work on his heart while he's under your employ."

"I hope so," Samantha agreed, her heart welling with compassion for a man who'd suffered through so much hardship in his life without recognizing that there was a merciful God willing to see him through. "I really do."

* * *

Will had first caught sight of Samantha when he'd spread out the picnic blanket underneath a sturdy oak on the green. He might not have been looking for her, but his gaze had been magnetically drawn to hers all the same.

Okay. Maybe he *had been* looking. A little.

Which was probably why he'd been so distracted that his four-year-old genuinely beat him at several rounds of slapjack. He certainly hadn't purposefully lost the games. He had too competitive a nature for that.

Samantha was standing in a line for fireworks, speaking with her friends, whom he now knew, from knowledgeable and perhaps slightly gossipy neighbors and customers, were called the Little Chicks. As he observed the three women, he could easily see how they got that moniker—he'd never seen three ladies so animated in all of his life. Most of the men in Serendipity no doubt found that quality—and those ladies—quite appealing and attractive, which he supposed they were, but he was scared to death of women like them—outgoing, constantly invading his personal space.

Samantha most of all. She invaded his emotional space, and that was far more frightening than a woman stepping too close to him. Will knew her heart and her generosity, and for those reasons and more, he *did* find her attractive and appealing.

Better for him if he felt nothing.

Better for *her*.

"He who finds a wife finds a good thing, and obtains favor from the Lord," Grandpa Sampson remarked. He slid into a lawn chair near where Will sat watching Genevieve playing tag on the green with some of the other children.

"I'm sorry?" Will cleared his throat, attempting to erase the pure astonishment he knew was threatening to reveal itself.

"No need to hide it from me, son," Grandpa Sampson said with a hoarse chuckle. "I've seen the way you've been lookin' at her when you think no one's watching."

Will groaned inwardly. If Grandpa Sampson had noticed, others probably had, as well. His emotions were laid bare, and he'd never felt so uncomfortable, so vulnerable, in his life.

He shifted his gaze to the ground and picked at a piece of grass. "As you know, I've been married, sir. I wasn't very good at it."

"Perhaps," Grandpa Sampson remarked, "you just hadn't found the right woman. Yet."

Will couldn't let himself go there, even in his thoughts. It wouldn't be fair to Samantha.

"Just think on that, son."

Samantha was quickly approaching, and Will

cleared his throat to alert Grandpa Sampson to that fact.

The old man just chuckled and leaned back in his seat.

"Check out what I just bought," Samantha said. Will moved onto the edge of the blanket to make room for her. She upended a canvas bag touting the Sam's Grocery logo, and a pile of fireworks—mostly fountains and multicolored boxes of sparklers—spread out before him in the middle of the blanket. "There will be a nice fireworks display at the end of the evening," she explained, "but folks around here like to entertain themselves while they wait."

"That doesn't sound safe." He suddenly felt like a Roman candle had gone off in his chest. "Is it?"

He'd thought they were only going to see a fireworks show put on by professionals—at a distance. And even that was going to be difficult for him. The sound of explosions, however innocent, could take him back to combat, to the war zone. Even if he was perfectly aware it might happen. Even if he tried to stop it.

Never mind *him*. If Samantha thought he was going to let his little girl play with a stick glowing with ashes, much less a fountain of sparks, then she didn't know him as well as he'd thought she did.

"Take a breath, Will," Samantha murmured, laying a warm hand on his arm. "I promise I would never do anything to put Genevieve in danger."

Will nodded and tried to even his breath, but it was difficult with his heartbeat roaring in his ears. He *did* trust Samantha. Of course she wouldn't allow anything bad to happen to Genevieve. He didn't yet trust himself as the guardian of a young one, but he could bank on the fact that Samantha would always put a child's needs ahead of her own.

"You didn't exactly answer my question," he reminded her. "Can't the grass catch on fire from the sparks?"

Samantha gazed across the park as if the thought had never occurred to her. "I suppose it *could,* but to be honest, in all of my twenty-eight years, it's never happened that I know of. Besides, the entire volunteer fire company is out here tonight with their families. Even if there was an incident—which I truly believe is highly unlikely—they'd be on top of it before anyone even knew it happened. But if it makes you feel better, we can set the fountains off along the pathway." She pointed toward the gravel path that wound through the community green.

Will swallowed hard. He knew he was about to sound like an overprotective mother hen, but he had another question to ask her. "What about burns?"

Samantha gave him a strange look. "I'm sure the occasional burn happens, but probably to reckless teenage boys who use the fireworks improperly. Surely you remember being a young, invincible risk-taker."

Will had actually never experienced fireworks as a child, or even as a teenager. His father hadn't been much for celebrating national holidays, and his mother was too timid to stand up to him. By the time he was old enough to rebel, his father had made the habit of locking him in his room.

Young and invincible had not really been part of his makeup as a teenager.

He shook his head.

"No? Well, regardless, when used correctly, I promise you fireworks are totally safe."

His gaze met hers, her blue eyes completely earnest. For a moment, there was such concern in her gaze that he suspected she guessed what was really going on.

"Trust me?" she whispered.

His gaze shifted to Genevieve, who was playing tag with a group of children near her own age. It amazed him how children naturally flocked together if given the opportunity to do so. They just found one another, and they welcomed newcomers into their midst. School hadn't even started yet and already she was making friends. He was so proud of her. And he figured he had Samantha to thank for that.

Obviously fireworks were a longstanding community tradition here, and he didn't want to give in to his desire to take his daughter and get out before he disappeared into his memories of Afghanistan. He could see the smiles, hear the laughter, smell the aroma of grilled hot dogs and hamburgers that made his mouth water. This was a full-blown party. He was the only one who appeared to be having qualms about it. Even Amanda and Samuel hadn't batted an eyelash when Samantha had dumped her load of fireworks onto the blanket.

He'd have to work to shut out the phantom sounds of gunfire and mortar blasts and remind himself that the noise and laughter around him were coming from a happy occasion.

He reached deep inside himself to find new strength. Just because he was had issues didn't mean Genevieve ought to have to suffer along with him.

He realized he would do anything for his precious little girl.

Absolutely anything. Including fireworks.

"Will?" Samantha's voice penetrated into his thoughts and he could tell from her tone that it was probably not the first time she had called his name. He suddenly realized she was touching his arm.

He tried to smile at her but knew he hadn't succeeded in the endeavor. She frowned back at him.

"Where did you go?" she asked softly.

Will considered deferring her question rather than answering it, but then she slid her hand down his arm and placed it in his, giving him a reassuring squeeze. Suddenly he found that he wanted to share the truth with her. He just wasn't sure if he could.

"It's okay if you don't want to do the fireworks," she said before he could speak. "I can give them to one of the other families. There will still be plenty for Genevieve to see, even if we don't participate ourselves."

"No. You're right. We should let Genevieve do her sparklers. I'm making a big deal over nothing."

She narrowed her eyes at him. "Don't tell me it's nothing."

He forced a laugh. "I feel that I ought to point out to you that just a few moments ago, you were arguing the opposite side of this conversation."

She tilted her head, looking thoughtful. He waited for her to say more.

She didn't.

Neither did he. So much for sharing the truth with her.

"Hey, Monkey," Will called affectionately, rolling to his feet and tousling Genevieve's hair as she came running up to greet him. "Miss Samantha bought us some sparklers. Do you want to do one?"

"Yes, please." Her big brown eyes gleamed with excitement.

"Red, green or gold?" he queried.

"Red. Red is my favorite color."

Will paused in the middle of reaching for the green box. "I thought you told me your favorite color was green." He'd been mentally filing all the useful information he'd been learning about his daughter, and he was positive she'd said green was her preferred shade. Just the other day she had insisted on wearing a poufy green skirt with a Christmas-tree green shirt and green ribbons in her hair.

"Red is my *new* favorite color," she informed him in a distinctly female tone of voice.

Apparently the entitlement of a woman to change her mind on a whim wasn't learned behavior.

"Miss Samantha's favorite color is red," Genevieve explained.

"Well," Will drawled. "That explains it, then."

Samantha giggled right along with Genevieve. The sound made Will's heart happy.

"So how do you go about lighting one of these things?" He opened the red box and slid one of the sparklers into his hand.

Samantha's surprised gaze met his. "Are you serious? You've never done a sparkler before?"

Will shook his head.

"Oh," Samantha murmured. "I'm sorry."

"For what? It's not your fault my father was an overbearing jerk."

Samantha knelt before Genevieve, wrapping an arm around the girl's shoulder and pulling her close. She adjusted the sparkler in Will's grasp so the safe end was in his fingers and then placed Genevieve's hand over the top of his wrist. Time seemed to slow as he savored the feel of his hand, and his daughter's, enfolded in Samantha's grasp. His chest welled so tightly he thought it might burst from emotion. There was something inherently right about the three of them united in this way.

"There we are." She nodded in satisfaction and reached for the long-stemmed candle-lighter in the picnic basket. "And here we go!"

She lit the end of the sparkler. The stick glowed and then sparked brightly, popping and crackling. He didn't care for the sound, but he relaxed when he saw the glow of the firework reflected in his daughter's eyes. Her happiness was worth any price—and any amount of discomfort on his part.

Samantha was clearly enjoying the child's delight as well. She was sharing it, really. He'd never met a woman who embraced the moment the way Samantha Howell did, with such joy and vivaciousness. He envied those qualities. She absorbed the life around her, lived in the moment. He was a man who struggled to find any kind of joy or peace in his existence at all, although it was getting easier with Samantha and Genevieve in his life.

Jo Spencer, the boisterous elderly redhead who owned the local café, approached waving a lit multicolored sparkler in one hand and a miniature American flag in the other, reminding Will of the conductor of a symphony. She was wearing a T-shirt proclaiming *Like Freedom? Kiss a Soldier.*

Will's breath caught in his throat as Samantha's gaze met his. Despite all his good intentions and resolve to keep himself away from Samantha—at least in *that* way—the T-shirt triggered a smile. If the deep rose color rising to her cheeks was any indication, she was aware of Jo's T-shirt, as well, and her mind had gone exactly where his had. There was a certain satisfaction in that.

"Isn't this absolutely the most enjoyable time of year?" Jo asked merrily.

Samantha chuckled. "You say that about every holiday."

Jo looked taken aback for a moment, but then she burst into high, melodic laughter. "I do, don't I?"

Samantha nodded and winked at Will, making his gut flip. Repeatedly.

"Well, at least this gives you all the opportunity to get out and put aside all that nonsense about the town council meeting with Stay-n-Shop. It's this coming Friday night, right?"

"What did you say?" Samantha bolted to her feet, a stricken expression on her face.

Will's adrenaline pulsed to life. He could hear his heartbeat pounding in his ears as he waited for Jo's answer. Cal had mentioned approaching the town council, but he hadn't known they'd actually scheduled a date. And neither, apparently, had Samantha.

"Oh, my dear, I'm so sorry," Jo said, raising her palms to cover her cheeks. "I let the cat out of the bag, didn't I? I didn't realize the council hadn't contacted you yet. My bad."

Will was fuming. She'd better believe it was *her bad.* He had no idea how this woman could have possibly discovered this information before the Howells even had wind of it. Didn't the town council have to contact *all* of the parties involved before they went and made a public agenda? He was steaming mad, not so much at Jo as at whatever person or entity had dropped the ball on this one.

"When's the meeting?" Samantha's jaw was set, but her voice was surprisingly steady and even.

"This Friday evening, if I'm not mistaken. I can ask Frank about it to make sure."

"Do you have any idea what their agenda is?"

Will was amazed at how well Samantha was taking the news. She was calm. Collected. Rational. *He* was the one who felt like throwing punches, like running pell-mell across the green screaming his outrage at the top of his lungs. What kind of a mixed-up, backward legal system was this?

"That I do not know," Jo said, responding to Samantha's question, and in an odd sort of way, Will's unspoken one. "I'm surprised you've had no contact with Stay-n-Shop, seeing as you'll be the competition should they decide to build here."

So much for her not knowing anything.

"I only heard there would be a meeting, nothing specific," she continued. "I'm sure you'll be contacted soon enough, dear. Oh, my, I hope I haven't gone and ruined your celebration."

"No. Of course not." Samantha managed to smile, although Will couldn't imagine how. "We appreciate you coming by."

And accidentally body-slamming us, Will added mentally. Samantha might be able to smile through the pain, but he didn't have that much strength.

"How did she find out about this before we did?" he whispered harshly the moment Jo was out of earshot. His throat felt as dry and gravelly as the path beneath them.

"From her husband, Frank, I imagine. He's the president of the town council. Jo is a sweet lady, Will. She didn't mean anything bad by it."

Samantha turned to him, her beautiful blue eyes glistening with unshed tears. Will's heart snapped. He couldn't bear to see her in pain.

He reached for her shoulders to steady her, but she misinterpreted the gesture and stepped forward into his arms. She fit comfortably there. He could rest his cheek on her hair and inhale the floral scent of her shampoo. She was as delicate as a flower yet as strong as a rock, and she was absolutely amazing.

"It'll be all right, honey. I promise," he whispered into her hair.

She tensed for a moment, and then she leaned back to look at him, her gaze softening, baring her vulnerability. He knew how difficult it was for her, admitting she needed someone—that she needed *him*.

Something about holding Samantha close to him strengthened his own resolve. No matter what, he would not let her be hurt.

Not by Stay-n-Shop.

And most especially not by him.

Chapter Nine

The Howells called a meeting of their own, a family council right there on their red-plaid picnic blanket on the green. The fireworks show had not yet started, and most of the folks around them were celebrating with their own kin. Genevieve had wandered over to where their neighbors Ben and Vee Bishop were lighting off fountains and Vee was watching over the girl, which was just as well because Genevieve didn't need to see Samantha as worked up and angry as she was.

"We need a plan of action—*now*," Samantha announced to her family. They were hovering, looking concerned even without knowing the whole story. She crouched in the middle of the circle like a quarterback in a huddle.

"The enemy has advanced," Will murmured, a sarcastic bent to his tone.

"What do you mean? What changed?" her father asked.

"Apparently, Stay-n-Shop has already scheduled a meeting with the town council for next Friday night. Jo Spencer mentioned it. She seemed surprised that that was the first we'd heard of it."

"Count on Jo to be the *very* first to know," her mother murmured with a chuckle that sounded half like a hiccup. Samantha knew how hard it was for her mother to contain her emotions under this set of circumstances. Samantha was feeling the same things—confusion, anger, fear, pain.

"Their calling a meeting can only mean one thing," Will ground out.

"They are proceeding forward with obtaining the zoning and permits necessary to build their store on that land they optioned," Samantha finished. "I don't think they're targeting Sam's Grocery anymore. At least not directly."

"Pardon the cliché," Grandpa Sampson offered, "but it sounds to me like we've just stepped out of the frying pan and into the fire."

Adrenaline set every one of Samantha's nerve endings alight. If it had come down to fight or flight, as it appeared to have, then they were most certainly going to fight.

"Let's take it down to the bare truth of the

matter," Will suggested, his jaw clenched. "We need help. Lots of it."

"What kind of help?" Samantha was disinclined to beg, even from the town council. Their family couldn't afford a lawyer. Besides, Matthew MacPherson was the only practicing lawyer in Serendipity, and he specialized primarily in family law, not anything like this corporate fiasco.

Cal Turner had been right in that respect. This issue was way out of Matthew MacPherson's sphere of expertise.

"We get our help from Serendipity itself," Will answered simply. "The answer is right here." He made a sweeping gesture across the green.

"What?" Samantha asked.

Will looked at her as if she was being dense and completely missing the point. Maybe she was. Or maybe she just didn't want to hear it.

"If we're going to fight this, we need to get Serendipity behind us. We need to prove that everyone supports Sam's Grocery. Stay-n-Shop can't battle the whole town. They'll most certainly see the futility of their move and go bother someone else, somewhere else."

"But what if they just go target a family like ours in another town?" Samantha asked.

Will's gaze widened and then he shook his

head. "You know I didn't mean it that way. I wouldn't wish Stay-n-Shop on my worst enemy."

"Stay-n-Shop *is* my worst enemy," she mumbled.

"*Our* worst enemy," Will corrected, his gaze daring her to deny it. She glanced around at the rest of her family, who were all apparently in agreement with Will's statement.

"So what exactly are you proposing we do?" Grandpa Sampson asked, his voice gruffer than usual, bringing everyone back to the heart of the topic.

"Let's circulate a petition. Tonight. Right now, before folks get caught up in the big fireworks show. Once that gets cracking, we're going to have a harder time keeping people's attention."

"And this petition would say…?" Samantha asked.

"Something like, 'We, the undersigned, object to the building of Stay-n-Shop within Serendipity town limits.' Then we can say a little about how everyone is supporting Sam's Grocery."

Samantha shook her head. This didn't feel right. She couldn't ask her friends and neighbors to put their necks out on the chopping block on her behalf. It wasn't fair to them. "That's putting people in quite a spot, don't you think?"

"How do you mean?"

It was Samantha's turn to gesture around the green. "I've known most of these folks all of my life." She paused, pulling in a breath that audibly hitched in her throat. "And before you ask, I will tell you that most of these people *are* regular customers at Sam's Grocery, and always have been."

"I know. I've seen them around," Will agreed. "They're good, loyal customers to the core."

"But maybe they wouldn't be, given a choice." Why was she the only one who could see it?

"What are you trying to say, Samantha?" her father demanded. He leaned forward in his chair, bracing his elbows on his knees.

"If we stick a petition in their faces, they'll feel obligated to sign it, even if privately they might be interested in the variety and discount pricing a big-box store like Stay-n-Shop would offer. It's hardly fair to make them choose between being a good neighbor and feeding their families. Besides, it's not like we can expect anyone to sign a petition without first being given the opportunity to mull it over."

"I disagree," her mother said, slapping her palms against the plastic arms of her chair. "If folks wanted big-box stores, they wouldn't live here in Serendipity. There is a difference between free enterprise and old-fashioned family values. We're a small town with a nice country grocery. No one will want a change as big as Stay-n-Shop would bring."

"Plus, time to mull things over is a luxury we don't have," her father added bluntly.

"Honestly, I don't think the folks around here will need to give this much thought," said Will, crossing his arms over his chest, which only served to make him look more muscular and solid than he already was. And more intimidating, if that's what he was going for.

Samantha was unsettled by the thought of imposing herself on her neighbors by springing a petition on them at the Fourth of July celebration. But maybe it was the only way.

She looked at each member of her family, trying to decipher their gazes and identify their take on Will's suggestion. Everyone was watching *her,* waiting with hopeful anticipation on their faces.

Suddenly she understood. They were waiting for her to call the next play. Talk about pressure. Especially from Will, who'd come up with the idea in the first place. Didn't he realize he was pushing his agenda on her when she wasn't yet prepared to accept it?

In Will's defense, this quick tactic was in response to the fact that they *were* out of time.

She sighed. "Where are we going to find some blank sheets of paper?"

"Give me a minute," her mother said. "I think I have a few sheets of crafting paper in the trunk of my car." Her brow lowered and she pursed her lips. "I'm afraid it might be pink. I was working on a shower present for Ben and Vee's baby girl."

"Never mind the color," her father insisted with a dismissing wave of his arm. "This is an emergency. Let's go, go, go."

Her mother caught Samantha's gaze and rolled her eyes before heading off to her car. "Pink paper isn't going to look very professional," Samantha felt inclined to point out.

"Neither is the fact that we're handwriting the petition. We'll be okay, as long as it's legal. And even if it isn't, pages full of names protesting Stay-n-Shop should count for something," Will replied, tunneling his fingers through his hair. He looked like he was ready for action, ready to take on the world for Sam's Grocery. For *her*. Seeing him like that made her stomach do a little flip.

When Samantha's mother returned, she had several sheets of paper, which were, to Samantha's dismay, baby-shower pink.

"Let's make several copies of our petition, and then we can each canvass a different area of the green. That way we can get as many signatures as possible in the shortest time possible,"

Will suggested, his voice strong and level, and that of a man used to leading. "I'm sure folks will have a lot of questions, but we have to do the best we can and move quickly."

Samantha still wasn't sold on the idea, but in the end, she took the sheet of paper assigned to her and started her way around the outside of the green. She and Will were working clockwise, while her mother and father were moving counterclockwise, one member of the team on the outside of the green, and the other canvassing the middle. Grandpa Sampson had been charged with staying put to keep an eye on Genevieve.

Samantha approached Zach and Delia Bowden, who were picnicking with their three children. She took a deep breath, kneeling next to Delia, before plunging in. She was fully aware that her pride was standing in the way of godly humility, but she couldn't seem to get past it. She wasn't one to put out her hand for charity, even when she needed it—as she did now.

"What are you selling?" Zach teased when he spotted the paper and pen in her hand. He cradled their sleeping six-month-old baby, Faith, against his shoulder, while his two-year-old son toddled around on the grass. "Candles? Cookies? You've caught us too late for candy. We've just had dessert." With his free hand, he patted his lean midsection.

Samantha blanched. Was she that transparent? She wasn't certain she could get a single word out. Not about Stay-n-Shop, or any other subject, for that matter.

Zach's words kept echoing through her head. *What are you selling? What are you selling?*

What choice did she have? If she stayed on the road she was currently going down, what she'd be *selling* was Sam's Grocery.

Delia, a longtime friend, put her arm around Samantha's shoulders. "Don't mind Zach. He's just being a goof."

"I—I," Samantha stuttered, and then coughed. "Need your help."

"You've got it," Zach stated, before she'd even said a word to explain what it was that she needed.

"Don't you want to hear what I've got to say before you commit yourselves?"

"Sure. You tell us what it is you're asking," Zach said with a mischievous grin. "But that doesn't change the fact that we're going to do anything in our power to help you out. Whatever you need. Just name it."

Samantha gave a shortened version of the facts—Stay-n-Shop's plan to build, their option on the land, the town council meeting. She didn't see the need to mention the pressure she'd been receiving from the corporation, or the threats.

"We're circulating a petition requesting that the town council rule for Stay-n-Shop to take their business elsewhere. Of course, there are benefits intrinsic in a big-box store, especially for a large family like yours—"

Zach chuckled. "Are you trying to talk us out of signing?"

"Zach!" Delia reprimanded, reaching for the petition and the pen. "Don't give Samantha a hard time right now."

"Just teasing," Zach said, taking the petition from his wife and adding his own name to it. "You know I'm just ribbing you, right, Samantha?"

Samantha nodded and smiled in gratitude. "Thank you. This means more to me than I can say. And to my family, as well."

"You don't have to thank us," Delia responded. "We love Sam's Grocery. We would never dream of shopping anywhere else. And neither will any of your other customers. Trust me on this one, Samantha. You have nothing to worry about."

"We're all behind you one hundred percent," Zach added, gently rocking his sleeping baby.

"Delia's right. You have nothing to fear. The town council will back you one hundred percent."

"I certainly hope so," Samantha agreed. She thanked them again and moved on to the next family. Maybe the Bowdens were right. Maybe all her apprehension was for nothing.

She could only hope and pray that was so.

She moved on. The next family she encountered was Chance and Phoebe Hawkins, along with Frank and Jo Spencer.

Even though it had been Jo who'd brought the council meeting to her attention, she was a little nervous approaching the Spencers. After all, Frank presided over the town council that would ultimately decide the fate of the store.

But Frank was surprisingly gracious, especially considering how gruff the old man usually appeared. He recused himself from signing the petition, of course, but wished her the best.

Frank's courtesy gave Samantha confidence to approach others on the side of the circle she'd been assigned. With each family she encountered, her spirits rose. Everyone she spoke with signed her petition and encouraged her in the endeavor. She'd been afraid she would be pressing folks to sign a petition before they were sure what they were signing, but it quickly became evident that the community not only wanted to support the store, but more importantly, wanted to champion Samantha and her family.

"How'd it go?" Will asked when they met back at their picnic site. They sat down side by side on the blanket to compare notes. Genevieve ran up and sat down on Will's lap with a squeal of pleasure.

Samantha was flushed with excitement as she displayed her hastily prepared petition. "They all signed it," she said in grateful amazement. "Every one of them. I can't believe it."

"I can," he said, showing her his own page, also brimming with signatures. "These people care about the grocery." He leaned back on his hands so his mouth was close to her ear. "And you."

A ripple of pleasure went through her. Somehow she had the impression he was speaking of more than the community's support.

"The fireworks should be starting soon," she said, observing the twilight sky. She glanced down just in time to see a dark expression flit across Will's face.

"Will? What is it?" she asked softly.

"Huh? It's nothing," he denied.

She scooted closer to him so they wouldn't be overheard. "I understand if you don't want to talk about it, but there's clearly something wrong. I'm a good listener."

He sighed. "I know you are. I just don't like to talk about it."

"The war?" she guessed. It was either that or his failed relationship with Haley, and he'd already talked to her about that.

The first firework popped in the sky, and Will flinched, despite the fact that he was clearly trying not to.

"Oh," she said, suddenly understanding why he was so reticent about the fireworks. "I'm so sorry, Will. I wasn't thinking."

"I'll live," he said through gritted teeth. "I'm one of the lucky ones. I only have a mild case of PTSD."

"Still, if you'd like to go, we could just call it an early night."

Genevieve clapped in delight. "Oh, Daddy. Look at that one. It's a red-and-green flower!"

"Your favorite colors," Will said, kissing the top of his daughter's head. "Cool, huh?" He smiled weakly at Samantha. "I can't miss this, now, can I?"

"You're very brave," murmured Samantha, slipping her hand into his and giving it a comforting squeeze. His hands were so large, so strong, and yet for his daughter, he was exposing the cracks in his defense.

Samantha had never been more attracted to a man in her life. What was it about a man that was so incredibly appealing?

Whatever it was, Will had it in spades, and Samantha found her own defenses dropping. She leaned closer and threaded her fingers through his, lending him her strength.

He smiled tenderly down at her. His hands were no longer trembling.

Chapter Ten

Will bagged the last of Chance Hawkins's groceries with his usual care and precision. Funny—helping the folks in Serendipity with their grocery shopping needs had become his favorite part of the job.

Working as a unit supply specialist in the Army wasn't nearly as fulfilling as bagging cans of baby food and toddler treats. He'd take small-town service any day of the week. It wasn't so much stocking supplies—it was supplying people. And not just with material goods, but with a friendly countenance and a helping hand.

He was beginning to recognize most of the folks who shopped regularly at the grocery, and he had the natural gift, which Samantha had complimented him on more than once, of up-selling to his neighbors. They always walked away with a candy bar and a smile.

He couldn't imagine anything better than being here in Serendipity, working at Sam's Grocery. He'd finally found his own little spot in the world, and he and his daughter had a real home at last. He had a sense of peace he'd never experienced before, knowing that what he was doing made a difference in people's lives.

His work at the grocery. His side job doing carpentry for the Howells' soon-to-be-opening bed-and-breakfast. He enjoyed helping them out with various and sundry jobs, and he was almost as excited as they were to participate in the grand opening of their new venture.

He was especially gratified by the community's response to the Howell's petition. It was an honor just to be a part of it. As for his time with Samantha—well, all he knew was that he'd never before experienced such strong emotions for a woman. It defied words.

For once, his life was wonderful. His daughter was happy, safe and secure.

Which would last for about five seconds, if Stay-n-Shop had their way.

He hated that some large, impersonal corporation was threatening to take everything he cared about away from him. From all of them.

The town council meeting was tonight at the Grange hall, and everyone was talking about it. As Will had suspected, most everyone had been anxious to sign their petition, and from what he was hearing, the council meeting was going to be full to bursting with folks wanting to give their opinions on the issue.

The only ones who'd recused themselves were the council leaders themselves, and Will wondered if they'd formed their own judgment on the matter already. Were they weighing both sides of the issue? Was it possible that the town council felt like the Stay-n-Shop could actually be a good development for Serendipity, economically speaking?

And what about Cal? Would he be leading up the offense at the town meeting? There was no doubt that the man was compelling and enigmatic. He might be able to sway the council members. The thought made Will feel sick to his stomach.

At the end of the day, they were Serendipity residents, and had been all their lives. That had to count for something. Small-town life was the status quo. It was what they lived and believed in and had always known. Sometimes change *wasn't* the best thing. What was the old saying? If it ain't broke, don't fix it?

Sam's Grocery wasn't broken. It was a central part of folks' lives in Serendipity and had been since the town was first built. Will firmly trusted that was the reason the town council would vote in favor of keeping Stay-n-Shop as far away from Serendipity as possible.

He wished he were a praying man. Maybe now was the time to start.

"Ready for the council meeting?" Chance Hawkins asked, as if reading his thoughts. Will realized Chance could probably see the tension on his face and guess where it was coming from. Will corrected his expression. He shouldn't be frowning at customers, especially those as regular as Chance Hawkins.

"I think so."

"Looked to me like you got a lot of signatures the other night at the Fourth of July celebration."

"We did. Nearly everyone was ready and willing to sign our petition."

Chance planted his black cowboy hat on his head and lowered it over his brow. "Of course they were. We're a country town. And for Phoebe and me, and my aunt Jo, too, that's the way we want to keep it."

"I'm glad to hear it."

"We've got a babysitter lined up for tonight, so we're all planning to be there at the Grange to support you."

That was an answer to a prayer Will had never actually prayed. The more people they had there in their favor, the better off they'd be.

"And thanks for digging out those little juice

boxes from the back. My toddler, Aaron, won't drink anything unless it's out of a straw."

"Glad to do it," Will said as Chance tipped his hat and headed toward the door.

He *was* glad to do it, and happy to be right where he was. He whistled as he grabbed a broom to sweep the front porch. But as he stood on the rickety wood-planked sidewalk and stared down the street at the old, clapboard-style shops and businesses, he paused and wondered if everything he had here in Serendipity was about to go away, thanks to the Stay-n-Shop.

Could he stand it if it did?

If worse came to worst, he could give up the grocery, and his job, and even where he lived.

But he couldn't give up Samantha.

He was too far gone and he knew it.

But he had no idea what he was going to do about it. The last thing a woman as remarkable as Samantha Howell needed was to be saddled with the likes of him.

Even so, he couldn't get what Grandpa Sampson had told him out of his head. His words echoed as if they'd been thrown into the depths of a canyon.

He who finds a wife finds a good thing.

A wife? When had his heart and his mind turned from just surviving day to day, to finding the permanence he was so desperately seeking?

Was there even the remotest possibility that he would have another chance at life, at happiness?

...and finds favor with the Lord.

There was the rub, for if God was present in the world, and Will was beginning to think He might be, Will knew in his heart that he didn't deserve God's favor. There was no way he ever would, for he could never make things right.

Samantha could not stop pacing. She had piles of paperwork to go through, but she couldn't seem to sit still and concentrate. She was fidgeting all over the place, both in mind and body. She wouldn't have a comfortable moment until the city council formally announced their decision to turn Stay-n-Shop away with a firm *no, thank you*.

"Ready to face the dragon?" Will asked, popping his head into the back room. He was wearing a determined smile and a baseball cap that shadowed his eyes, but she was certain she saw a twinge of doubt in his gaze. Whenever he was on edge, his eyes turned very nearly black, as they were now.

She remembered how mysterious—and frankly, intimidating—he'd appeared when she first met him. She hadn't been able to figure him out back then. His stoic attitude had locked her out.

But now she could read him. She understood his body language—the way his jaw tensed or his brow creased when he was troubled. The clench of his fists that confirmed the words he could not or would not say aloud.

But there was the other side of him, too. The kind, gentle side. He didn't often display it for the world to see, but she'd caught glimpses of the man he was deep down in his heart, and the man he could become—the smile on his face whenever Genevieve kissed his cheek, the adoration in his gaze when he called her Monkey and ruffled her hair.

And sometimes, there was something special in the way he looked at her and drew her into his world. Those were the moments Samantha loved most of all.

But the expression on his face now was sheer and complete resolve. Her heart sank.

"We aren't going to win this, are we?" she murmured, laying a hand against his chest to feel the steady beat of his heart. He closed his hand over hers, pressing it to his chest.

His eyebrows rose. "Of course we are. We've talked about this. The whole town has got your back. Stay-n-Shop can't fight everyone."

"I hope you're right."

Will moved behind her and gently massaged

her shoulders, rubbing his thumbs into the knots at her neck. His hands were large, warm, strong and supportive, all the things she needed right now.

Where would she be if Will had not come into her life?

He'd changed everything. He'd spurred her to action. He'd helped her make things happen. And although she was still facing her giant, she was no longer alone in her fight.

"Are we on the docket?" she asked him.

He chuckled dryly. "Honey, we *are* the docket."

Samantha frowned. "If they cleared the agenda just to talk about this one issue, they must be anticipating that it will take some time."

"If you ask me, it's just a bunch of red tape," Will responded. "They're obligated to hear what Stay-n-Shop is proposing before they can officially send them packing. Word on the street is that many of the prominent businesspeople in the community are planning to attend the meeting in person."

"That makes me even more nervous. It's going to be all I can do to keep it together while I counter the corporation's arguments, even without having half the town present to see me falter and fumble."

"They'll all be there to support you. And to watch you win."

She folded a piece of white paper into a small box and then flattened it onto the smooth oak desktop with her palm. She only wished it was as easy to crush the big-box store. "You make it sound like a sure thing."

"That's because it is, honey. It is."

That evening, the Howells gathered at Samantha's parents' house so they could all travel to the Grange hall together and enter with a united front and one purpose in mind.

Winning the war.

Samantha put on her best Sunday clothes, a soft white cotton dress dotted with a colorful variety of Texas wildflowers in purple, blue, red and yellow hues. She imagined she would look like a country bumpkin up against the slick corporate lawyers in their New York suits made by designers Samantha had neither heard of nor cared to know.

They were probably counting on that—the intimidation factor, the big-shot businessmen sanctioning their presence in the tiny country town.

What they didn't realize was that *she* was the one with the hometown advantage here. Surrounded by Serendipity folk, the Stay-n-Shop representatives wouldn't fit in. That realization made her feel a little better.

She thought of Cal Turner with his slicked-back black hair, deceitfully charming smile and forceful intimidation tactics, of how he'd tried to force her hand and make her sign papers to make her family legacy go up in smoke.

Now Cal Turner was bringing friends.

Well, she had friends, too.

She glanced once more in the mirror to check her appearance, added a brush of pink gloss to her lips and decided it was as good as it was going to get. She hurried to the living room, where Will was waiting, dressed in a white cotton shirt and black slacks. He'd even gone so far as to wear a necktie, although he kept fidgeting with it as if it was choking him.

She saw him first, and she knew without a doubt the moment he realized she was in the room. He stood abruptly, his eyes wide with admiration. His appreciative gaze took in her white summer sandals and her cotton dress.

He gave a low wolf whistle and brushed his hair back with the palm of his hand.

"Wow." It was only one word, but it was enough.

Samantha shook her head playfully, but inside her heart was pounding in response. Who needed a bathroom mirror when she could see herself so much more clearly—and honestly—in Will's appreciative gaze?

"You clean up very nicely yourself," she teased, giving him a backhanded compliment that she meant with her whole heart. "I can see you've ironed your shirt." She ran a finger down the carefully pressed crease from his shoulder to his wrist. "You know what they say about men who wear ironed clothes?"

Will arched a brow. "Enlighten me."

"Either they're in the military, or they still live at home with their mamas." She was grateful for this small snippet of conversation that didn't have anything to do with Stay-n-Shop. Will seemed to understand that she needed that brief step back, and he played along.

"I see. Really? Do *they* say that?"

"Absolutely. And seeing as you don't live at home with a woman pampering you and seeing to your every need," she continued coyly, walking slowly around him and enjoying the view of his strong jaw and broad shoulders, "you must have been in the military."

Will shook his head and chuckled again. "Well, that must have been an awfully difficult conclusion for you to arrive at, since you've known I was an ex-soldier since the very first time we met."

Samantha's heart was beyond warm. It was glowing like the glimmer in Will's eyes. He was *teasing* her. He had progressed so incredibly far from that poker-rigid man she had first met.

"Samantha," he murmured huskily, reaching for her hand and turning her toward him, stepping forward so they were face to face, so close she could feel the brush of his breath on her cheek.

"You and your theory got one thing wrong," he whispered close to her ear.

"Yeah? What was that?" she asked through the hitch in her throat, her voice suddenly unable to function beyond a whisper.

"I *am* home."

His words struck her with the force of a hurricane, yet it was everything he couldn't say—all of the emotion burning in his eyes as he continued to hold her gaze—that sealed the deal for Samantha.

He reached for her other hand, his touch all at once strong and gentle.

This man belonged in her life. And after this whole mess with Stay-n-Shop was over and their lives were back to normal—or at least the new normal—she would tell him so.

Will's forehead met hers, his luminous brown

eyes glittering with unspoken promises. "Samantha, I—"

Grandpa Sampson appeared in the doorway and cleared his throat. Will jumped back, clasping his hands behind him.

"I hate to interrupt what looks to be quite the interesting moment," Grandpa Sampson said with a gruff chuckle, "but we gotta get ourselves out to the Grange hall and kill us a bunch of snakes."

Samantha looked at Will, who seemed to be as thunderstruck as she was, plus a little guilty, too.

What did he have to feel guilty about? She was the first to admit that her grandfather catching them mooning at each other like a couple of lovesick calves was a little embarrassing, but their stance hadn't exactly been compromising. They were only holding hands, not kissing or anything. And even if they were, she was twenty-eight years old, not an immature adolescent.

If she wanted to have a relationship with a man—and the word *relationship* wasn't even close to defining whatever it was she had with Will—then that's exactly what she would do. Will's support had become a cornerstone for her. She'd grown to depend on him. No—more than that. She'd grown to *care* for him. But right now they had to face the present crisis. And Grandpa Sampson was right about one thing.

It was time to kill some snakes.

Chapter Eleven

Will's heart was still spinning from his brief encounter with Samantha. He felt like she'd taken him to the craggy edge of a towering cliff with white-capped surf below it and then, with a single fingertip, was about to push him over the edge.

It was a good thing Grandpa Sampson had come in and interrupted when he had. Will had—completely, inappropriately and with the worst timing ever—been right on the verge of kissing Samantha.

Where was his head? Why could he not keep his emotional distance from this woman, no matter how hard he tried?

Here they were, ready to go into the legal battle of their lifetimes, a battle that would mean all the difference in the world not only to Samantha personally but to all the Howells and to him and Genevieve, as well. This was the time for him to be putting on his mental armor, gearing up for the fight ahead, not ruminating over his sudden penchant for Texas wildflowers.

"I'm not sure exactly how we should expect this meeting to go," Samantha told her family, who'd all gathered in the living room. "I've only been to a couple of town council meetings, and they weren't about such touchy subjects or burning issues. I think the last one I attended had to do with building an official preschool in Serendipity."

"I've been to a few," Samuel remarked. "They're basic at the core, run pretty much like a board meeting at a business—Robert's Rules and all that."

Grandpa Sampson snorted. "Like any of us have the first notion about Robert and his blooming set of rules."

"It's just to keep order, Grandpa," Amanda said soothingly. "No need to get all het up about something we can't control. Anyway, I imagine it's probably not so formal as all that."

"Well, I still say they didn't give us enough time to prepare. Them corporate fools have been working on this a long time, and I'll bet *they* know Robert's Rules."

"The council is only required to give us three

days notice," Samuel said. "And they gave us five. So we've nothing to complain about."

That wasn't exactly true, Will thought as he watched Samantha grimace. Had she been honest from the get-go and brought the situation with Stay-n-Shop to the family from the very first, they would have had much more time to prepare a case as a group. He knew what she was thinking. She was blaming herself. She was thinking that if anything, *she* was the one guilty of springing this on them.

Obviously, she'd never intended for the matter to go this far. He was certain that if she'd known Stay-n-Shop wouldn't take a simple no for an answer, she would have shared her problems with her family right away.

As it stood now, well, it was what it was.

"Why don't we focus on what we do know," Amanda suggested gravely.

"Right." Samantha jumped in, clearly seeing this as an opportunity to move the conversation forward. They didn't have much time before the meeting started, and they needed to talk last-minute strategy. "There are currently eight commissioners on the board. Most if not all of them are either small businesspeople who own a shop somewhere on Main Street or are kin to those who do."

"Which means, theoretically, there could be

a tie vote," Will said, surprised by this new information. "Has this happened often?"

"Not often, no," answered Samuel grimly. "But it has occurred occasionally, usually in the higher-profile cases. In some cases, they've argued for a week of Sundays before coming to an agreement on an issue. On rare occasions, they've hung themselves out to dry."

"So what you're saying, then, is that we need to win five commissioners to our side," Will said.

"Yes. Precisely. That shouldn't be so hard. Should it?" Amanda started her sentence firmly, but by the time she tacked on the ending, she didn't sound quite so certain of herself.

"Stay-n-Shop is slated to present their case first," Samantha informed them. "I'm expecting them to come in ready to impress, with algorithms, statistics, presentation software and who knows what else."

"Which could work against them," Will pointed out.

Samantha met his gaze with a grateful look. "Exactly what I'm hoping will happen. Folks around here, the town council members included, might not take to all the fancy show of equipment and ideas. Perhaps they'll be more open to our simple plea, our show of integrity over industry."

"So they do their blabbing, and then Samantha, you give them the petitions with all the signatures on it and set them down the right path," her father said.

Samantha sighed. "I don't mind working with folks when I'm behind the counter at the grocery," she said. "It's easy for me to be outgoing when I'm serving people. And I know I have a reputation as a Little Chick," she continued, scoffing and shaking her head. "But in truth, public speaking is so not my thing. I'm scared out of my gourd right now."

Will reached for her hand, feeling her fingers quivering under his. He wished with all his heart he could take her place, or at least take away her nerves, but this was one battle she had to captain on her own.

"You're going to do great, honey," he murmured. "True courage isn't not being afraid. It's facing your fear and going forward anyway. And don't forget, the Lord will be with you every step of the way."

Her gaze flew once again to his, her eyes wide with surprise. "Yes, of course. Thank you."

He realized after he'd said the words that that was probably not the best advice, at least not from him. He didn't want to give her any kind of hope that he was coming around to view the world as she did. He knew she was praying for him, that he'd become a Christian, but he still didn't know where he stood with God. Certainly they weren't in good standing with each other. But he'd reminded her of the Lord because he knew it would help *her*, and ultimately, he supposed that was all that really mattered.

The Howells also looked grateful for Will's timely reminder.

"Will is right. We should pray," Samuel suggested, "and ask the Holy Spirit's covering over us as we march in to face our enemy tonight."

Will was already holding Samantha's hand. It seemed like the most natural thing in the world to thread his fingers through hers as they gathered in a circle to pray. Will bowed his head and closed his eyes with the rest of them, but his prayer was a little different than theirs.

Where Samuel prayed for peace and wisdom for the members of the town council, Will hoped Samantha would be persistent, no matter what the council's immediate impressions might be, what kind of day they might have had or what they might have consumed for breakfast. It seemed to Will that there were too many variables to lay anything as serious as this at the feet of eight different people. Better to focus their prayers on Samantha.

Samuel prayed for the grace for Samantha to find the right words, and Will hoped she'd be able to find the strength to speak so convincingly and forcefully that no one on that tiny country board had any niggling doubt of what the right decision was.

And hopefully, that would be the end of story. Happily ever after, at least for Samantha and the Howells.

He was a new man since arriving in Serendipity. Samantha had shown him his own strength and given him courage when he'd thought he had none. She made him experience emotions he hadn't even believed existed.

For him, this was only the beginning.

Samantha was shaking so hard her teeth were chattering against each other. She inhaled deeply through her nose, willing herself to calm down, although she didn't know how she was going to do that when every nerve ending in her body was screaming. The muscles in her neck and shoulders were so tight she could hardly turn her head to look at Will, who was beside her, his arm loosely draped around her shoulders as they stood outside the door to the Grange hall.

He smiled his encouragement and used his fingers to massage away some of the tension at her nape. She wondered if he could feel how tightly she was wound up or if it was just that he could see the sheer panic in her eyes. If he could see it, so could the rest of the world.

"Ready?" he whispered, leaning close to her ear.

"Not really," she said, chuckling without humor at her lame attempt at a joke. "I wish I could blink and make all this just go away."

"Me, too, honey. Me, too. But I've learned that sometimes the only way to get to the other side of something is to just muck it up and go through it. I think tonight calls for some major mucking."

"Well, I ought to be pretty good at that. I spent most of my summers visiting friends on their farms. I've mucked my share of stalls."

Will nodded and kissed her temple. "Then go to it." He gestured toward the parking lot, which was full of trucks and cars, mostly of the working variety. "Seems to me that half the town's already here, and every one of us has got your back."

"I know you do." She couldn't quite shake the sense of guilt that hovered over her like a storm cloud. If she hadn't been so proud and arrogant and believed she could handle Stay-n-Shop all on her own, things might never have escalated to this point in the first place.

Now it was time for her to fix what she'd broken. Despite everything, her family still believed in her and supported her. She desperately wanted to regain their trust. It went without saying that to do that, she needed to secure the future of Sam's Grocery.

Will was right. It was time for her to buckle up and settle this. It wasn't going to go away on its own, not with all the praying and hoping in the world. For whatever reason, God had her right here, right now, facing this particular giant, this threat to her whole way of life. She just hoped that she'd quickly learn whatever lesson it was He was trying to teach her so she could score a victory for Sam's Grocery and her family. And for Will and Genevieve.

"Here goes nothing," she muttered as she pushed the door open.

Up until that moment, Samantha had been aware of the low but distinct murmuring of the crowd inside the little Grange hall. But at the sound of the door opening, every head turned to face her and talking instantly ceased. With chairs set up in rows like the pews in a church, she felt like a bride at her wedding, except it was all the nerves without any of the joy.

She knew all these people. The ironic thing was that they *were* the folks she would invite to her wedding. Alexis and Mary were sitting in the second row on the right. When the time came, those two women would be her maids of honor—both of them—and she was grateful for their support now.

If only this was a happy occasion.

What was it Will had said? That courage wasn't lack of fear, but knowing fear and acting anyway?

At least she had Will at her side. As she walked up the aisle in what she hoped looked like a confident manner, she continued to breathe in and out through her nose, slowly, methodically. If she held her breath, which was what she tended to do when she was nervous, she would pass out. If she breathed too quickly, she would hyperventilate and then pass out. So the only way she was going to stay cognizant, never mind focused, was to carefully monitor the air coming in and out of her lungs.

As she expected, a gaggle of Stay-n-Shop legal representatives were clustered near the front. Cal Turner, with his stylish suit and confident demeanor, was among them, though he didn't immediately glance in their direction. The other legal experts had paused briefly when Samantha and her family had entered, but now they were huddled together around a rectangular folding table on the left, covered with notes and laptops, presumably discussing strategy for the upcoming meeting. A similar table, devoid of anything, had been set up on the right for her and her family. She and Will slid into the chairs behind the table, while her family filed into the first row behind them.

Samantha looked down at the single file clutched in her hand. Even if she spread out every single page of the petition, it wouldn't even cover half of the tabletop. And she didn't even own a laptop, other than the one that belonged to the grocery. Now, however, she wished she'd had the foresight to grab it from the office. It didn't have any notes or anything on it, of course, much less a fancy presentation to share, but at least it would have looked nice and official on the bare table. This wasn't a formal courtroom, but it certainly felt like one.

Carefully avoiding the competition, her gaze swept across to the very front of the room, where, upon a small stage, the town council members sat, facing the house full of people. Samantha scanned the faces, all of them familiar to her, including old Frank Spencer—Jo's husband—the man officially presiding over the night's events.

Those sitting on the council flashed Samantha friendly smiles and her nerves settled. These were her people. Many of their kin had signed one of the petitions Samantha was holding in her hand. Surely they would bring a swift and satisfactory conclusion to this muddle created by a big-box store that had no business in a small country town.

But what if they didn't? Who could say what the outcome might be?

Samantha once again focused on her breath and reminded herself that ultimately it was God overseeing this assembly. In His mercy, He knew what was best for her, and for Sam's Grocery. She just had to trust in that.

Frank Spencer banged his gavel—which was nothing more than a regular hammer probably taken from his tool box at home—three times against the surface of the table, and waited for the ruckus to die down.

"I'm suspecting that this here is going to be a long meetin', so let's just set our policies straight from the get-go," he said. "Number one, I'm the one who was elected president of the town council, and that means I'm in charge, so you don't get to do no talkin' unless I've cleared you to."

So much for Robert's Rules of Order, Samantha thought, allowing herself the tiniest of smiles. *More like* Frank's *Rules.* She'd known old Frank Spencer her entire life. He was a cantankerous old goat, but he had a good heart, and he'd keep the slick corporate guys from getting too high on their horses.

"Second," Frank continued, "there will be no outbursts from the peanut gallery." He gestured to the people in the house. "That means you, folks. No cheering, booing, clapping or anything else. Got it?"

Samantha glanced back to see several people nod and murmur, but the room fell to complete silence when Frank narrowed his gaze and pointed his hammer toward them.

"Third, this meetin' will be held in an orderly fashion. First, y'all from the city get to state your case. Then," he said with a brief nod toward Samantha, "it'll be your turn to go. After that," he continued, waving his hammer in another authoritative gesture toward the house, "I'll give you folk a few minutes to voice your opinions for this council to consider."

When it remained so silent they could hear a coyote howling in the distance, Frank flashed a self-satisfied grin. "Now then, I'm going to introduce the council members one by one and allow them the chance to introduce themselves to you."

Samantha really didn't see the point in that. It wasn't like the townspeople didn't know the eight folks sitting behind the bench. She supposed it was done for the sake of the Stay-n-Shop lawyers, or maybe it was only for show. Either way, Samantha took a moment to compose her thoughts, as ready and as prepared as she could be for whatever Stay-n-Shop would throw at her. Her family was seated in the first row of chairs behind her, but Will, seated in the chair next to her, reached for her hand under the table and gave it a brief squeeze.

"Go ahead when you're ready," Frank said to the corporate lawyers as soon as introductions were complete.

Samantha shifted her attention to Cal Turner as he rose with a flourish and began to speak.

"Ladies and gentlemen," he began, directing his first remarks to the town council.

To Samantha, he sounded very much like a ringmaster at the circus. She half expected him to add *boys and girls* to the start of his speech. *Welcome to the greatest fiasco on earth!* All he needed was a top hat. She wanted to scoff. Instead, she clasped her hands together on her lap and dug her fingernails into her skin, concentrating on the pain in order to help her keep her mouth shut. She reminded herself that she'd have her turn soon.

"In consideration of all the folks here tonight," the lawyer continued, turning to address his first remarks to the house full of townspeople, "we'll keep our remarks brief and to the point. I know you all have families to go home to, and that is exactly why we're here. We at Stay-n-Shop know that you treasure your families deeply, and we're here to make a difference in all your lives."

There was an answering murmur, to which Frank put an immediate stop by threatening to pound his gavel.

"We here at Stay-n-Shop put family first. We promise you the deepest discount on the biggest variety of fresh, frozen and general-use products in the grand state of Texas."

Samantha had positioned her chair so that she might be able to see the reactions of at least some of the house, and met the gaze of Edward Emerson, who owned the hardware store. Selling general-use items would cut into Ed's business, as well. He scowled and shook his head. He wasn't any happier hearing about this than she was, and it was probably the first time he'd been fully informed.

She recognized her own failing once again of putting her pride over the genuine needs of others. She was certain she'd be hearing from Ed, and maybe others who ran businesses on Main Street, about her appalling lack of communication. Come to think of it, she was surprised she hadn't already.

She had expected the corporate lawyers to play the *family* card, but not as their leading argument. If they knew the town as well as their statistics said they did, they would know that "family and faith" ought to be their final and most significant argument. In half a minute, Cal Turner had ticked off all the reasoning Samantha had anticipated from him. At this rate, he'd have nothing left to say in a couple of minutes.

As it turned out, though, that wasn't even remotely close to the truth. She should have figured that Cal Turner would milk every statement into a variety of subpoints, and then back up each and every one of them with colorful graphs, charts and other relevant data. Samantha had to admit that their analysts had done an impressive job serving up statistics on how Stay-n-Shop had positively affected the economies of those country communities where they'd built new stores. Not only did they offer discounts, but perhaps more importantly, they provided jobs, which were valuable commodities in any small town.

Worse yet, Cal was a consummate professional when it came to speaking to both the board and the room full of townspeople. Clearly he spent a great deal of time in courtrooms in front of judges and juries, and it showed with every word that came out of his mouth. His voice was warm and rich, with the hypnotic timbre of a lullaby. His strong presence was definitely going to be a point in his favor, even without all the numbers—*dollar signs*—backing him up. He knew just when to make a gesture with his hands and what expression to wear upon his face. Through it all, he appeared affable and approachable. The bottom line was, Cal could read his audience like a book. Or rather, like a snake waiting to attack its prey. Any time he perceived interest from the townsfolk, he would press whatever issue was currently at hand right into their laps. Rather than causing them to back off, it appeared to be subtly urging them forward.

She gazed across the crowded room, noting the number of people whose expressions registered interest in what Cal was saying versus those whose body language was clearly of the opposite persuasion. Chance Hawkins, slumped in his seat with his arms crossed firmly over his chest and a scowl low on his dark brow. His wife, Phoebe, her arm draped affectionately around him, wore equal disapproval on her face. Jo Spencer was wearing a T-shirt scribbled with the words *Robert's Rules,* on which *Robert's* had a line slashed through it and had been replaced by *Country.* Now that was more like it.

But others were obviously not so quick to decide. Doubt or intrigue was written on their faces. She could hardly blame them. Cal Turner, with all his bells and whistles, was making a flashy argument, the likes of which this tiny town council had probably never seen before.

So much for an open-and-shut case.

This was going to be harder than she'd imagined.

Didn't these folks realize they were like frogs in a pot of water warming to the boiling point?

Cal began wrapping up his speech by addressing the board. "As you can see, ladies and gentlemen, Stay-n-Shop will be entirely beneficial to Serendipity and the surrounding communities. We offer any number of advantages, not to mention the jobs we will create in your economy."

He paused just long enough to slide Samantha and Will a triumphant grin. Samantha's stomach roiled when she met the man's eyes. Polished, charismatic Cal Turner thought he had her community in the bag.

Not if she could help it.

"In addition," he went on, "we at Stay-n-Shop promise to work for the good of the community. As you may know, our corporation regularly contributes to a number of nonprofit organizations, and we try to keep the money within the communities where our stores exist. We are standing here tonight ready to make a real difference in your lives and in the lives of all who reside here in Serendipity."

Cal smiled and nodded his head toward the board, taking his time meeting each and every one of the council members' gazes. He then turned to the people in the crowd, some fanning their faces with the agenda page they'd received, and spoke his last words.

"Stay-n-Shop. Discount. Variety. Charity. And employment. Thank you for your time."

Chapter Twelve

Will watched in silent admiration as Samantha composed herself. She had such beauty and strength within her. He knew it wasn't easy for her to step up in front of her community and ask for assistance. She was a brave, proud woman who would rather work things out on her own than be a burden to another. A woman who protected her family at any cost, always thinking of others before herself.

She was a giver, not a taker.

But this time she needed to take all she could get.

He was rooting for her with his whole being, supporting her with every nerve ending in his body on edge. And—what?

Praying for her?

He doubted God would listen to a man with the kind of destructive past he had, but perhaps

He would make an exception if Will's petition was on behalf of Samantha. At least she was a genuine believer, and strong in her faith.

He'd heard enough prayers during his time visiting the Howells to be able to mimic their style, which he assumed was the correct way of approaching the Almighty. Since he had no other example in his life, he figured he'd give it a shot.

Lord, give her the right words to say. Keep her future safe. Let her feel Your presence and give her peace.

Lightness washed over him. He was praying for Samantha, not for himself, and yet he suddenly had the strangest impression that peace was growing and flourishing in his own heart. It was the oddest sensation, one Will had never before experienced and couldn't have explained if he was asked to do so. He didn't know what to do with it. It was emotion, and yet it was something far more than that.

Rattled by the phenomenon, he did what he always did when emotion threatened to overwhelm him and overpower his thinking—he willfully tamped it down and put a block over it, pushing it into the deepest recesses of his heart, where he no longer had to deal with it.

Eventually, perhaps, he would examine those

feelings. Later. Samantha needed him to have a clear mind right now.

Samantha approached Frank and handed him the file. They bent their heads together and spoke in low tones. Will couldn't make out the words, and he knew their opposition couldn't, either. She appeared to be pointing out various items to Frank, and he was nodding vigorously.

"Excuse me," Cal interrupted in a loud, authoritative voice. He stood and placed his fingertips on the table. "If there is a change in the agenda, I believe the correct procedure is for me to be advised. May I step forward and join the council?"

Frank shook his head. "No, you may not. This ain't no powwow. And it ain't a secret, either, from what I can gather." He tapped his palm against the pages of the petition. "It appears most folks are perfectly aware of what's going on here."

"What, exactly, has been presented without my knowledge?" Cal asked, raising one dark eyebrow and sounding both aggravated and exasperated at the same time.

Will had to restrain himself from cracking up at the way Frank Spencer was stringing the big-shot lawyer around. He was positive Frank was doing it on purpose, just to make a point that he was the one in charge.

Samantha turned, addressing both Cal and the crowd, gesturing to include the council members in her speech.

"Folks, you all know me and my family, and you know what I stand for. My great-grandfather was an honest-to-goodness Western pioneer, the very Samuel for which Sam's Grocery is named. Ever since the day he opened his general store to serve the community of Serendipity, our country store has strived to meet the needs of everyone who lives here."

There was a wide-ranging murmur of consensus among the crowd until Frank threatened to bang his hammer again.

Good going, Will thought. One point to Samantha for mentioning her service to the community. *Now bring it on home, sweetheart.*

"It hasn't always been easy. Just like you all, we've had our fair share of struggles. But Sam's Grocery has prevailed through the ups and downs Serendipity has experienced, and we're still here and thriving and ready to serve our community. I hope we can continue in that capacity for many years to come."

Come on, Samantha, honey, give it all you've got. Will pressed his palms into the tabletop and his heels into the floor.

"To me, Sam's Grocery is more than just a store. It's all about people, personal service, family, tradition, history and legacy." Her voice cracked and Will could see her fingers quivering. Agonizing emotion and excruciating tension were a powerful combination. When she tried to resume her speech, her words came out as half a sob.

Will was on his feet and by her side within seconds. He didn't know how these proceedings were supposed to work, whether or not others were allowed to speak at this point, nor did he care. Robert, or Frank, or whoever was leading this shindig could throw his book of rules out the window, because he had something to say.

"When I moved to Serendipity after my tour of duty in Afghanistan, Samantha and her family graciously allowed me into their hearts and their lives. They provided me with a job so I could support myself and my daughter, Genevieve—they permitted me the very great privilege of working at Sam's Grocery."

He slipped his arm around Samantha's shoulder, steadying her and hopefully reassuring her as they turned to face the council members who would ultimately make the final decision.

"I'm here to tell you what Samantha cannot. Working at Sam's Grocery has been an eye-opener for me. It has changed my perspective in more ways than I can name—and all due to Samantha Howell. You all know what to expect when you come into our store—personal service from someone who genuinely cares about your well-being, who knows you and your family by name and can anticipate your needs."

"Hear, hear," called a deep voice from the crowd. Will thought it might be Chance Hawkins, a theory that was confirmed when the man added, "They always special-order boxed juice just for my son."

Frank leveled a gaze at Chance. "We'll have no more of your outbursts. You folks will get your opportunity to talk in a minute, so zip it."

Will released a deep breath. At least Frank hadn't told *him* to sit down and shut up.

"Here's what you're going to get at Stay-n-Shop," Will continued. "The store will be sterile and sanitized and not personalized in any way, except with its fancy end-caps designed to sell you more goods. No one will personally come to your service unless you search for an associate and ask for it, and even then, it'll be a starched transaction. There won't be anyone by your side to discuss the pros and cons of red versus green grapes or to assist you when your children get unruly.

"Opening a big-box store like Stay-n-Shop will bring a whole lot of new people into town. At first glance, you might think that looks like a good thing, economically speaking. More people means more money being spent around town, at our very own businesses.

"But think about this—more people means more houses being built, more land being developed. The possibility of more large corporations setting their sights on our little town."

Will directed his gaze to each of the member of the town council. He had their attention, all right. Their rapt attention. For once, even Frank wasn't muttering under his breath.

"I ask you—where does that leave Serendipity? What happens to the small, intimate community you now call home? I brought my daughter to this town to get away from all the trappings of the city. In my opinion, it would be a shame to bring them here. We already have what we need right here, right now. A country store with tradition and values.

"I say we stand by Sam's Grocery!" Will finished, his voice rising enthusiastically for the sake of the house.

This time there was a cheer, loud and long and buoyant, most definitely rooting for the little town store. Will grinned. He'd always known they'd have the community's support.

Samantha, too, was smiling, relief and thanks in her glittering gaze. She raised a hand, quieting the crowd. "I only have one last thing to say, and I say it with all my heart. I love this town. And I love each and every one of you."

She gestured to include everyone, but her gaze was on Will alone. His breath caught. He wasn't even sure his heart was beating.

And then, when she smiled at him, his heart roared to life, beating double time at the message in her eyes. Was he imagining it, or was she targeting her remark directly at him?

Was it all in his head, or was she saying she was in love with him?

Samantha had been more relieved than she could say when Will had stepped in to speak with her. Not *for* her—*with* her, lending her his strength both physically and with his words. He'd promised her that he'd have her back, and he'd come through on that oath.

There was no doubt in her mind that the assembly agreed with Will's well-spoken conclusions on the matter, if the cheering and hooting were anything to go by.

Frank called for order and begrudgingly opened the floor for comment. One by one, members of the community stood and shared what Sam's Grocery meant to them. Some shared personal stories about various times Samantha or her parents had been there to meet specific needs in their lives. Others spoke of the quality of the goods and the personal dose of customer service that went along with it.

Every observation was encouraging and in Samantha's favor. Frank didn't even try to stop that steamboat once it had pulled away from the dock. The entire council sat quietly, listening to the testimonies, sometimes grunting or nodding but saying little else.

"I call for a quorum," Cal demanded when he had apparently heard enough.

Frank turned his crusty frown upon Cal. Anyone else would have cringed, but Cal merely lifted his chin. "You can't call for a quorum. You aren't a member of this council."

"Then you do it," Cal challenged brutally.

Frank would have none of that, staring the overbearing lawyer down until he looked away. "I'll call for a quorum when I'm good and ready to call for a quorum, and not a moment before. Now sit yourself down there and be quiet."

Shaking his head and snorting at the implied insult, Cal reluctantly seated himself and started talking quietly among his cohorts. Samantha didn't even want to know what Cal was saying to his associates.

"I am, in fact, going to call for a private conference before I call for a vote," Frank said. "I believe this issue needs more discussion. The other council members and I are going to make use of that sweet Texas twilight so we can talk among ourselves and come to some kind of consensus on the matter. You all stay put until we get back." He leveled Cal with one last glare just for good measure.

The council members filed from the room, their expressions solemn. The knot in Samantha's belly tightened. These eight men and women were prominent members of the community, and all, like Frank, had auspicious and voluble opinions. It wasn't like them to be so quiet. Even Frank wasn't saying a word.

Maybe they had nothing to talk about. If it was already decided between them, at least in their own minds, then the end of this meeting would be quick and painless, at least for Samantha and her family. She'd be so incredibly relieved when the positive verdict came back and she could put this whole ugly part of her life behind her.

But what if they hadn't decided in her favor? What if Cal's presentation about economic development had won them over?

Friends and neighbors gathered around Samantha and her family, congratulating her on her speech and wishing her well. Alexis and Mary huddled close to her, loudly offering their forthright and not-so-nice opinions of Stay-n-Shop and Cal Turner and bubbling over with their love for her. Through it all, Will stood next to her, his arm still protectively draped over her shoulder as he spoke to Chance and Jo about how they thought the meeting had gone. Samantha knew that eventually she'd have to contend with her best friends' teasing remarks about her relationship with Will, but for the time being, she had no inclination to move away from the encouragement and strength he silently offered her.

Samantha looked around her at all the folks milling about and listened to the hum of their support. Her heart warmed as she realized how truly blessed she was to have a sympathetic community behind her. Her friends. Her family.

Will.

Had he understood the message in her gaze? Did he know how she felt about him?

"That went well, don't you think?" Will whispered, bending his head close to her ear. His breath was warm on her temple. "Take a look around. Everyone here is raring to go, to start celebrating our victory."

It did rather look like the folks of Serendipity were gearing up for a party, all smiles and laughter in every direction. Apparently no one thought Cal Turner and Stay-n-Shop stood a chance. Samantha's chest filled with gratitude and appreciation for everyone who'd taken precious time away from their families to come to her defense.

"Thank You, Lord," she murmured.

"What was that?" Will asked, leaning closer.

"Oh, nothing. I was just thanking God for His good gifts."

Will looked surprised. "But you haven't even heard what the council has to say yet."

She chuckled. "Don't you see? It's not about that." She gestured to the many people surrounding her. Supporting her. Loving her. "It's about this."

Will nodded, though he never took his eyes off Samantha. "Yeah," he agreed softly, his voice taking on a husky quality. "I think I do understand."

Cal Turner and his associates had taken the opportunity to pack up while they waited. Cal caught Samantha's gaze, his eyes still smug, still proclaiming the victory that he believed was his. He straightened his tie and grinned at her, and it sent a shiver down her spine, as if a diamondback rattlesnake had slithered over her shoe. She had the distinct impression from his black gaze that he enjoyed what he did, wrecking small-town dreams and messing with people's futures.

Samantha made sure her smile was secure.

As the minutes rolled on and there was still no sign of the council, Samantha started to worry.

The knot in her belly that had been there since before she'd walked into the room now started roiling with pierced, jagged edges. She felt a little shaky and wondered if maybe she'd accidentally been hyperventilating as her nerves increased. Only Will's firm arm around her shoulder kept her grounded as she leaned into him and consciously slowed her breathing.

"You okay, honey?" Will queried, his brow creasing.

"What do you suppose is taking them so long?" It felt good to get the words out, to share her apprehension with him.

The family gathered around the table and the folks from the community started returning to their seats. Surely a ruling was coming soon.

"Aw, it's nothing to worry about," Grandpa Sampson assured everyone. "Old Frank is probably jawing away about nothing out there. You know how he gets, especially if he thinks he's in charge of the operation."

"He kind of is," Samantha pointed out. *In charge of our future.*

"Well, then, that's a good thing for us, isn't it?" Her father's tone was firm and encouraging, but Samantha could still hear the sliver of doubt in his voice. "Frank would never dare vote opposite his wife or he'd never hear the end of it, and we all know which side Jo is on."

That much was true. When it was finally her turn to talk, Jo had taken the floor like a pro. She'd made no apologies when she ripped Stay-n-Shop all to shreds. She was like a mama tiger protecting her cubs, and in this case, the cubs in question were the Howells.

"All we can do is wait," Will said, giving Samantha's shoulder a squeeze. "There's no sense fretting until we know what we're going to be up against. But this may very well be the end of our fight."

"Or just the beginning," Samantha groaned. She wasn't sure her heart was going to be able to take it if she had to wait much longer. She thought her chest might explode from all the anxiety rocketing through her.

Just then, the council members started filing in the door and taking their seats behind the front table. Samantha tried to read their expressions, but none of them were giving anything away. Not *one* of them. And that's what was scary.

No smiles. No relaxed postures. Instead, they sat as still as statues and just as straight. The room was absolutely silent until Frank banged his hammer-gavel against the surface of the table. Samantha had no idea why Frank thought he needed to do that. He already had everyone's attention. Even the corporate lawyers seemed to be waiting with bated breath for the council's decision.

"I'm callin' this meeting back to order," Frank announced in his usual gruff tone. She tensed, waiting for the anvil to plunge down on her.

Will slid his arm from her shoulders to her waist and pulled her more tightly against him. Hip to hip. Shoulder to shoulder. She was not facing this moment alone.

"I'm sure everyone here knows just how important a decision this is," Frank began.

The crowd murmured in agreement.

"Our decision will affect not only the Howell family, but the community of Serendipity in general."

He paused and took a sharp breath of air before continuing. "As you must have surmised, the town council members here have carefully deliberated on the subject."

The hum of voices in the room dropped abruptly into silence, with Frank ready to make the life-changing announcement. *Pronouncement,* as far as Samantha was concerned. She could almost hear the collective intake of the crowd's breath. She was most certainly holding hers.

"What we've concluded," Frank continued, "is that it won't be fair to either party if we make a rash decision based on a few minutes of discussion. This is an extremely weighty matter. We are giving ourselves one week to think on it and deliberate some more. When we've come to a consensus, we'll directly contact the persons involved with our ruling."

Anger was the first of Samantha's emotions to set in, and adrenaline jolted into her system, bringing her nerve endings alive. She shook her head in protest. Stay-n-Shop wasn't a person. It was an entity. An unfeeling, impersonal entity with lethal steel-trapped jaws that were about to eat her alive.

"Just like all of the rest of you, we on the town council have known the Howells most all of our lives, so we understand just how sensitive this matter is. Naturally, it's difficult for us to be unbiased in our thinking, which is why we're taking a step back. Sam's Grocery has held a key position in Serendipity for a long time, and we're conscious of that.

"But allowing Stay-n-Shop to build their store in our area also offers folks some benefits we've not seen before within this township. We might not like it personally, but we've all acknowledged that there are both pros and cons to this scenario, and it's our duty to weigh them carefully and rule in the best interests of the majority. It ain't as cut-and-dried as all that, and like I said, we need more time to think on it. That's all I've got to say on it for now. Meeting adjourned."

There was a roar as the folks who'd showed up to support the Howells echoed their feelings of distress and outrage. They were clearly not happy with the outcome of the proceedings.

From across the room, Cal met Samantha's gaze and gave her a cold smile. As far as he was concerned, he'd won.

In a sense, he had. If the folks on the council had to think about it, that meant they were divided on the issue. And if they were uncertain, if there was even the tiniest sliver of doubt in their minds, Cal Turner would find some way to push his point home and urge the vote to his favor.

Samantha felt like someone had kicked her hard in the gut. Just when she'd started to believe that having the folks in the community behind her would sway the decision, she'd had the rug pulled right out from under her and had landed straight on her head.

And here she'd thought Stay-n-Shop might finally go away and leave them alone so they could move forward with their lives.

She was despondent and absolutely livid that

her reality had come to this. Economics versus legacy. Money talked. It screamed. The almighty dollar was twisting the life out of what was left of her heritage.

Discounts. Variety. Employment. Economic development. And what they had the nerve to call *charity*.

Really—who could fight with that?

She'd certainly put forth her best effort, but to no avail. Will had tried, as well, adding his own words to hers, standing up to the corporation and trying to show the people of Serendipity all they would lose should Stay-n-Shop enter their town.

The crowd had gotten the message, but the council, not so much. Had they even heard Will's argument against bringing a host of new residents to town? Or had they turned that reasoning on its head?

Samantha groaned and slipped out of Will's grasp. She was breathing so heavily she was seeing spots. She made a beeline for the door, desperately needing fresh air and a moment alone so she could pull herself together. She needed to see the stars in the sky to remind her of the Lord's presence and feel the soil below her to ground her to the earth.

She peered upward, trying to pray, but the

twinkling of the night sky was not enough. Because it appeared to Samantha that God had abandoned her in her hour of greatest need.

Chapter Thirteen

Will watched Samantha make a mad dash for the nearest exit, but despite the fact that he desperately wanted to follow her, he did not immediately spring up out of his seat. He'd seen her expression just before she'd turned away. She was struggling frantically not to lose it—at least not in front of other people. He well knew what it was like to need a little space to regroup, and he respected Samantha enough to allow her to gather herself before he came after her.

But it wasn't easy to sit and wait when she'd just been blasted by a life-changing emotional mortar, and all he wanted to do was find her and attempt to console her as best he could. He couldn't even begin to imagine what she was feeling right now, being told her legacy wasn't worth immediately upholding, and knowing nothing except that she'd have to wait longer to know for certain the direction her life was going to take.

He knew how *he* felt about it.

Actually, he didn't. Or at least he couldn't put words to the whirlwind in his chest that was causing his blood to roar in his ears. Flabbergasted might be close to describing what was going on. He had no idea how the town council could possibly see any true good coming out of soliciting big business. Did they not realize the ramifications of allowing Stay-n-Shop to build their store in Serendipity? How could they not have considered the many testimonies given by the folks who had come to support Samantha and the Howells, who felt Sam's Grocery was a vital part of their community?

Will decided he couldn't wait another second to find Samantha and take her in his arms and assure her that all would be well. That it would all work out in the end. With a determined set of his chin, he strode out the door. He had to find her and remind her that she was not alone.

It didn't take him long to discover where she'd gone. He found her slumped on the ground behind the Grange hall, away from the main doors and the parking lot where everyone else was heading. She sat with her back against the wall and her arms around her knees. Her head was resting within the crook of her elbow and her shoulders were quivering.

Was she crying?

Will's heart felt like someone was holding it in his fist and squeezing it. He didn't think for a moment that Samantha's tears showed any kind of weakness, but he didn't know what to do with a sobbing woman, how to make things better for her. It was killing him that there was nothing he *could* do for her to make things right in her world.

And there was the rub. As desperately as he wanted to, he couldn't help her. There was nothing he could do to make things better for her.

He crouched before her and tentatively laid a hand on her shoulder.

"I'm here, honey. Talk to me," he murmured.

Samantha didn't say a word. Instead, she rolled forward, wrapping her arms around his neck and burying her head in his chest. Her movement was so intense and unexpected that he nearly lost his balance. He caught himself and rocked forward onto his knees, cradling Samantha against him and allowing her to sob on his shoulder.

His heart ached for her. He desperately wanted to take away her pain, yet all he could do for her was hold her close, brushing his palm against the softness of her hair and soothing her with quiet words spoken lower than a whisper.

After a few minutes she stilled in his arms, no longer sobbing, but gasping heavily with a hitch in each breath.

He faltered for words. What could he say that would console her? What if he said the wrong thing, as he'd often done with Haley? What if he managed to screw things up, to make Samantha feel worse and not better?

"The answer isn't exactly *no,*" he finally stated softly.

Samantha used her palms on his chest to push back and meet his gaze. Her glorious blue eyes were shimmering with tears. Her mascara had run, leaving little streaks down her face and black smudges underneath her eyes. He rubbed them away with the pads of his thumbs. As he looked at her, he realized that Samantha was always beautiful to him, inside and out, no matter what. The thought thunderstruck him.

"It might as well be no," she countered. "You saw the look on Cal Turner's face when Frank announced that they were going to table the motion. If the council has to think about it, then it's not the open-and-shut case we had hoped it would be. And if it's not as straightforward as all that, the corporation has made their point.

They'll only push harder now that they know they have some leverage."

"We made our point, too, honey."

"Apparently not well enough. Do you think that all the talk about bringing in jobs and building up the town worked against us?"

Will felt like a crane's iron ball had swung around and knocked him in the head. *Had* his argument been turned on him?

"We still have to hold out hope," he responded firmly. "We have to believe that the council members will do the right thing. They are all longtime residents of our town. I'm certain that as they think it over, they'll see Stay-n-Shop for what it is—a threat to our small-town way of life."

"What if they don't? How do we know they aren't going to focus on the *benefits* of the big-box store? What if they see it glowing in marquee lights?"

Will sighed and shrugged. "I suppose we can't know for sure. But I do know who you can depend on completely."

Samantha looked at him expectantly. Will wanted to tell her that she could depend on him completely, but he knew better than to promise her any such thing. Haley had depended on him, and look what had happened there. No.

There was One far greater and more reliable than he was.

"Old Frank?" she guessed, thinking he was talking about the council members.

"I expect Jo will keep him in line, but I was actually referring to someone else."

"And that would be...?"

"God, of course. Ultimately He is the one in control, don't you think? He's going to bless you and take care of you no matter what the council decides."

Samantha remained silent, looking pensive.

"You've got your family," he reminded her. His voice turned raspy when he added, "And so far as I am able, you've got me."

She pulled him tighter, as if she was proving to herself that he was really here. She was practically choking him, but he didn't mind. He couldn't really breathe anyway, not when he was so aware of the moonlight softly caressing her face.

He *was* here. And he would be. Like he'd said—as much as he was able.

"Don't forget—tonight most of the community spoke up against allowing Stay-n-Shop to build."

"No. I won't ever forget what happened tonight. I'm forever grateful that all those folks cared enough to fight for Sam's Grocery."

Will chuckled dryly. "They weren't fighting for Sam's Grocery, honey. They were fighting for *you*." His heart welled with his own feelings for her. He cared so much that it scared him. "They were there for you and your family, and for our whole way of life in Serendipity."

"Our soon-to-be-changing way of life," she reminded him grimly.

"Maybe," he admitted, his voice deepening. "Or perhaps it won't make any difference at all, no matter what they build or don't build. You saw how many people came out for you tonight. Who's to say they'd even patronize Stay-n-Shop? Just because it might exist doesn't mean the residents of Serendipity will have to shop there."

"Not at first, maybe."

"Not at all," he assured her. "I imagine most folks are going to keep shopping where it's familiar and friendly, with the townspeople they've known all their lives—Sam's Grocery." He was determined to make her see his point, but she seemed equally determined to ignore it.

"Until they need something on a Sunday afternoon and they realize they can run over to Stay-n-Shop to get it. Don't you see? We can't compete in their arena. Once folks try it, they're bound to go back. Maybe not a lot at first, but as time goes on, our customers will start migrating toward the convenience of the big-box store, and my business—*our* business," she corrected herself, "will dry up and eventually blow away like dust in the wind."

"You can't think like that or you've already lost the war," Will insisted.

"Maybe I have. Maybe I should just concede now and cut my losses."

"What?" Will's voice rose both in tone and volume. That didn't sound like Samantha—like the never-give-up, never-give-in woman determined to protect her family and her town from Stay-n-Shop's bad influence. This was a woman who felt the obligation to take the whole world's problems on her shoulders just to keep others from having to suffer.

"It's just—"

"It's just *nothing*," Will interrupted her before she could finish her pessimistic statement. He cupped her face in his palms, forcing her to look him directly in the eye. "Don't you give up. Do you hear me? Don't you even think about it."

One lone tear rolled down her cheek.

"Look to God for your strength," he reminded her softly.

She sighed, leaning her cheek into his palm. "I know you're right. It's just the waiting I can't stand. I need a decision, one way or another, so I can move on with my life."

Her eyes gleamed so blue. Her skin was soft under the roughness of his hands. The floral scent of her shampoo was playing havoc with his senses, wafting around him and drawing him closer.

Her gaze was begging him to put an end to her misery. She needed something to remind her that there was so much good in Serendipity, so much good in her life.

She needed...

He needed...

"Will," she whispered, holding perfectly still as he closed the small distance between them. "I—"

He brushed a finger over her lips. "Shush. Don't say anything."

He slid his hand over her hair and cradled the nape of her neck, adjusting his arms around her until they fit perfectly together. His blood surged through his chest like a waterfall in a tropical paradise and he cherished the moment as his lips hovered over hers, their breaths mingling warmly together.

In the back of his mind, he was still aware of his guilt. He shouldn't be here. It wasn't right. He couldn't be the man that Samantha needed him to be.

Tomorrow that might be true, but at this moment, he couldn't be anything *but* what she needed him to be. He sighed and gave in to the inevitable, despite how long and hard he'd fought against it. He could no more stop himself from kissing Samantha than he could stop the stars from twinkling in the sky.

Her eyes were like those stars—glittering, luminescent.

"Samantha, honey," he whispered against her lips. It was his last conscious thought. Her soft mouth yielded to his, her lips giving and receiving. He wanted her to know his support. He wanted her to feel his love.

His grip tightened as he deepened the kiss, putting his whole heart into showing what he could not say, and knowing it was what she most wanted to hear.

I love you. And you are not alone.

Samantha ran a hand over Will's strong shoulder and sighed. Her other palm rested against the graze of whiskers on his jaw. It was wonderful to be in his arms. She hadn't realized until now just how long she'd been waiting for this moment—maybe from the first time he'd walked in the door of Sam's Grocery.

His kiss was at once gentle and demanding, soft yet intense. His arms surrounded her like a fortress, his shoulders a stronghold against everything bad and difficult in the outside world.

Nothing existed except Will—the solid strength of him, the enticing musk of his aftershave, the way he'd whispered her name in the passion of the moment.

He made her feel beautiful. Safe. *Loved.*

The unspoken, invisible bond between them was unlike anything she'd ever experienced before. Their embrace wasn't just a meeting of lips but the union of two hearts. She'd prayed about this moment from the time she was old enough to understand the nature of love, and she savored it with all that was in her being, because now she recognized those emotions tugging at her heart.

She was in love with Will.

Her heart was soaring. Will cared for her, too. She realized, looking back, that he'd been silently communicating his feelings to her for quite some time—protecting her from nearly the moment he'd first walked into her life. She'd simply misread the signals.

But now he was showing her how very much she meant to him in a way that was beyond misinterpretation.

He had to know she felt the same way about him. She put just as much meaning into their kiss as he did. But where Will preferred to convey his emotions through deeds and actions, Samantha needed to say the words. Out loud.

"Will," she murmured as he tenderly leaned his forehead against hers. "I want you to know that I—"

He seemed to freeze suddenly, and then bolted to his feet and backed away. The movement was so abrupt, so harsh, that Samantha, completely shocked, hardly knew what to do.

"Don't," he rasped, the single word a direct order. "Don't say it, Samantha."

"What?" she asked in bewilderment. Her mind was still muddled and cloudy from the kiss and her heart was still pounding in her ears. She felt like she was being plunged back into mental chaos after having a moment of pure, beautiful clarity.

Maybe she hadn't heard him right. That had to be it. She hadn't understood what he was saying.

"What's wrong, Will?"

"I think we ought to stop right here, before anything else happens."

"Are you kidding me right now?" she demanded.

He tunneled his fingers through his hair, leaving it pointed and disheveled, a mirror image of the way her emotions felt right now.

"We got caught up in the moment," he explained, his voice grim, a far cry from how soft and loving it had sounded just moments before.

"We were both upset. It happens. Let's leave it at that."

"It *happens?*" she repeated as her heart was pierced by the sharp edges of Will's words. "It happens. That's all you are going to say about it?"

She felt like a puppet. Will had jerked her strings and she had blindly danced to his music. And then in the next instant, he'd dropped her, leaving her in a mixed-up heap of parts on the floor.

Maybe Will was right. Maybe they *had* gotten caught up in the moment. Her stress level was through the roof, after all. Her entire life was falling apart. But in her case, the pressure had only forced her to admit what she'd already known deep down—that she had feelings for Will.

That she *loved* him.

He, on the other hand, was brushing those emotions off as if they were nothing. And yet he'd been the one who'd reminded her of all her blessings, who had encouraged her to lean on God during the tough times when she was beginning to believe she had nothing and no one.

For some crazy, wonderful and now absolutely mortifying reason, she had thought, at least for a moment, that she had Will.

What a fool she had been.

"So, what was that, then?" she hissed. "You were just stealing a kiss because I'm vulnerable right now?"

His eyebrows lowered over his smoldering eyes, which had turned almost black, as they always did when he was experiencing great emotion.

"Don't do that."

"Don't do *what?*"

"Don't belittle what we shared. It meant a lot to me."

She ignored his admission. He was just yanking her chain again, and she would have none of it.

"It seems to me that you're the one belittling what we shared. It also seems to me you're doing an awful lot of ordering here. You aren't in the Army anymore, Will, so don't tell me what I can and can't do."

"Please," he pleaded. "Don't diminish what happened here tonight. I care for you. I really do. But for reasons I can't explain, I can't go there with you."

"Can't? Or won't?" Maybe she was being unfair, pushing him further than he was ready to go, but she had to know the truth. He couldn't just kiss her like that—like he was ready to give her the world—and then step back and tell her he couldn't *go there*.

"Honey, I can't give you what you're asking me to give to you."

She felt like Will was taking a chain saw to her heart, methodically cutting it into smaller and smaller pieces until there was nothing left. "If that's true, Will, then why did you just kiss me like that?"

He looked at her for what felt like an eternity with those heart-stoppingly beautiful brown eyes that for once she was able to read clearly. She saw love in his eyes—she was sure of it. But she also saw fear, and uncertainty.

"I promised you that I'll be there for you," he said, his voice hard, even cold, "and you can bank on that promise. No matter what happens with Stay-n-Shop, I'll be by your side."

"Is that all this is to you, Will? Is this just about the Stay-n-Shop?"

"That's all it can be, Samantha. Trust me on this. Let's just focus on the Stay-n-Shop and leave the rest alone."

He turned and headed back into the Grange hall, leaving her right where he'd found her before he'd changed her world with a single kiss.

At the moment, she didn't give a fig about Stay-n-Shop. She wanted Will. She wanted *all* of Will, especially the one thing he apparently refused to give.

His heart.

* * *

"Hey, Monkey," he said as he scooped Genevieve into his arms, squeezing her extra tight and running his hand across her black curls. Holding his little girl in his arms was his anchor to reality right now. It was all he had.

"Thanks, Delia," he said to the woman hovering in the doorway. "I appreciate you watching Genevieve tonight."

"Anytime," Delia said pleasantly. "How did the meeting go?"

Will's mind immediately flashed to those moments after the meeting, when he held Samantha secure in his embrace. The most wonderful minutes of his life. And his biggest mistake of all.

"The Grange was filled to bursting with folks coming out to support Samantha and her family. I think it went well."

"I heard Stay-n-Shop brought in a whole legal team."

"They did. Hopefully the council will see through their arguments and keep Sam's Grocery safe."

"Tell the Howells I'm praying for them."

"I suppose that's the best thing we can do for them at this point."

"Daddy, you're holding me too tight," Genevieve exclaimed, wiggling.

"Sorry, Monkey," he said, bending to place her on the ground.

"Your daddy just loves you so much he wants to squeeze you like a stuffed animal," Delia said with a chuckle.

Well, that was true. And more. Genevieve was all he had. He didn't want to screw that up.

"Thanks again," he called over his shoulder as he buckled Genevieve into the car seat. Delia waved and closed the door.

"Are we going to see Miss Samantha?"

It was an innocent question, but it pierced Will's heart like a knife.

"No, sweetheart. It's late. Miss Samantha might already be sleeping." He knew she wouldn't be. Not tonight. Not after what he'd pulled with her. She was probably stomping around her house, mulling over his demise.

And rightly so.

"Miss Samantha promised to show me how to play the piano," Genevieve said.

Will's throat burned. "You really like Miss Samantha, don't you?"

"She's nice to me. And she's so pretty. You like her, too, don't you, Daddy?"

Will hadn't shed a tear since he was five years old and his father threatened to hit him if he didn't stop bawling like a baby, but at Genevieve's words, his eyes burned, and it took every bit of strength within him not to give into the urge to let go. It hurt that much.

He had to clear his throat twice to answer. "Yeah, Monkey. I like her, too."

Chapter Fourteen

Will hadn't seen Samantha in three days, and he hadn't slept in nearly that long, either. There was no doubt in his mind that she was avoiding him, and he supposed he really couldn't blame her. He'd hurt her—deeply—which was the last thing he'd ever meant to do. But now it was too late to take back what he'd said—or what he'd done.

On Saturday, Samantha's parents had asked him to take a day off from the store to finish building a wraparound porch for one of the cabins near the river. There was a certain satisfaction in building things up instead of tearing them down. As he set the planks, he'd listened to the gentle swoosh of the river gliding over large, pointed rocks, and to the birds singing what Will imagined to be praise songs from the trees. A rare black squirrel had even approached him when he got too close to the animal's home. He'd been impressed by the squirrel's angry chattering and apologized for disturbing him.

It was a peaceful scene, but Will had felt no tranquility in his heart. Not while things were so completely unresolved between him and Samantha.

He'd declined to attend church on Sunday. He was too confused and confounded to come up with a reasonable excuse for why he wasn't going, especially since he'd only just started attending at all, but fortunately, the Howells didn't ask. They merely wished him a good day and left him to his own devices.

He'd hoped giving Samantha a couple of days to cool off and pray would give her new perspective, but it didn't take him long to realize he was wrong on that count.

Sometime during the night on Sunday, Samantha had left an envelope taped to his door, which contained a key to the store and brief, scribbled instructions for him to go ahead and open the shop Monday morning on his own. He'd thought maybe she was running errands and intended to arrive late, but as the hours slowly passed, he came to the distressing realization that it was unlikely that she was going to put in an appearance at all.

He was able to handle the store on his own

with no problem, even with all the extra customers coming out in droves to support Sam's Grocery and bolster Samantha's spirits. He wished she could have been there to see the day's business, and thank the community that was well and truly behind the Howell family legacy.

Whether or not Stay-n-Shop was allowed to build on that land, Will firmly believed that Samantha's heritage was safe in the hands of the wonderful, faithful folks of Serendipity.

As the day ended and there was still no sign of Samantha, Will closed up, cleaned up and found himself reaching for his cell phone. He dialed Samantha's mother.

"Hello? This is Amanda."

"Hey, Amanda. It's me, Will."

"Hi, Will. I just fed Genevieve a bowl of macaroni and cheese. She said she was hungry and I like to spoil her a little bit when I can. She's like a granddaughter to me. I hope you don't mind."

"No, not at all." He was happy to hear the pleasure in Amanda's voice when she spoke of Genevieve. Samantha's mother and his young daughter had a special bond. They were good for each other, much in the same way that Genevieve and Samantha were good for each other. He pushed the thought out of his mind. "Actually," he continued, "Genevieve is the reason I'm calling. Or—er—part of the reason, anyway."

"Sure, Will," she said, sounding intrigued. "What can I do for you?"

"Have you seen Samantha recently?"

"I saw her yesterday. She played the organ for church, but she left right afterward. Why? Did she not show up for work this morning?"

"No. She left me the key to open with, so I figured she was going to be late, but she never came in at all. I thought maybe she was spending the day with you all. I guess she needed some time alone."

"That's odd."

Will sighed. "No, not really. I'm fairly certain she's avoiding me. She's not picking up her phone, either. Do you have any idea where she was upset?"

To her credit, Amanda did not ask what Will had done to upset her daughter, even though he'd pretty much admitted that was exactly what he had done.

"You really care for her, don't you?" she asked softly.

Everything in him burned—his eyes, his throat, his heart. He wasn't sure he could speak, but Amanda was waiting for an answer.

"Yes, ma'am, I do."

"So? What are you waiting for? Writing in the clouds?"

Will chuckled. "That would be nice."

"Indeed it would, but love is never that simple, or that tidy. We're all a mess inside, you know. Every one of us carries baggage. But when God unites two hearts, they can lift each other up, carry their loads together."

"But I—"

"Love my daughter. Go get her. Try the church. Ever since she started learning music as a little girl, the church has been kind of like her refuge. Playing the organ seems to help her organize her thoughts and work through her feelings about whatever is bothering her."

Which would be me.

"And before you ask, I'm happy to watch Genevieve for you for as long as you need me to."

"Thank you, ma'am," he said, gratitude welling in his heart. Once again, he was astounded by the Howells' continued generosity toward him. They just gave and gave without a second thought.

He could see where Samantha got her heart from.

"It's my pleasure," Amanda insisted. "That's what family does. We step in and help each other."

Will's throat clogged with emotion. He ended the call and then just stood staring at his cell phone.

Had she just referred to him as *family?*

He didn't know how that had come about, but it made him want to stay in Serendipity more than ever. It would be such a shame if he had to walk away from the best thing he'd ever known. If only he could make Samantha understand that no matter how much he loved her—and he did love her—he would not risk hurting her the way he had hurt Haley.

It was *because* he loved her, because he'd never experienced anything remotely close to the bond he had with Samantha, that he had to back away from the relationship. If he had to, he would even go so far as to leave Serendipity, but he hoped with all this heart that it wouldn't come to that.

Amanda had reminded him that everyone carried scars, perhaps even regrets, and that if he could get past his troubles, Samantha might be waiting at the end. But he felt so weighed down by his past. Could he ever let it go?

He heard the organ long before he actually entered the sanctuary of the church. Samantha was playing a dark, brutal piece of music that immediately reached into his soul and tore pieces away, leaving every last nerve vibrating with tension.

If her selection was anything to go by, she wasn't even remotely close to getting over being angry with him for starting what he couldn't finish, not that he'd expected her to be.

Now it was time to explain.

The last majestic chord of the piece set him off balance and he had to shake his head to try to regain his mental focus.

"'Toccata in D Minor'," she said as she slid from the organ bench and approached him. "It's Bach."

"It's chilling is what it is," he countered. He didn't know who this Bach guy was, but he sure wrote unsettling music.

She leveled him with a glare. "It *is* a little cold in here."

Well, at least she was honest—and she wasn't talking about the music or the air-conditioning. It was a place to start.

"I came to apologize," he said bluntly.

Her expression didn't change, yet Will felt her shift in emotion just as clearly as if she had burst into tears.

"I'm not here to apologize for kissing you, so let's get that clear right off the mark."

Her shoulders sagged, but Will didn't know whether it was from relief or dejection.

"Kissing you was the best moment of my life."

"Me, too, Will," she said, crossing her arms as if she needed to protect herself from him somehow.

"Along with the day Genevieve was born, of course," he added.

"Of course," she agreed, the sad smile on her face showing him that she knew exactly how important his daughter was to him.

She understood. She *got* him.

And he was going to walk away from all that? His brow furrowed. He considered himself a strong and powerful man, but did he have the fortitude it would take to do what was best for Samantha, even if it wasn't best for him?

She reached out and brushed a hand along his shoulder, bringing him back to the present.

"What are you not telling me?"

"I've told you everything. I can't ever be in a relationship with you. I won't. I'll hurt you, and I never want to do that. Don't you see?"

She frowned and shook her head. "See what, Will? What is it that you think is going to happen if you let yourself be with me?"

"I'm dangerous, Samantha. It's my fault Haley is dead. If anything were ever to happen to you because of me, there's no telling what I'd do." He took a deep breath, and finally let the rest spill out. "I don't deserve you, or your love."

Samantha took a step back, stunned not only by the words Will had uttered, but by how vehement his tone had been. His eyes were dark and reproachful—he was condemning himself.

Criminal, judge and jury. Guilty as charged.

But how could he say that, much less believe it?

Samantha stayed very still, as if Will would disappear if she made the wrong move. She ignored the very strong urge she had to wrap her arms around him and tell him what an amazing man he was. "Will, it's not your fault she's dead."

He leveled her with his gaze, cold and accusing. "Isn't it?"

"No, it isn't. You can't blame yourself for what happened in a dark alley a continent away from where you were at the time."

"Haley wouldn't have been in Amarillo working as a waitress in a truck stop if we hadn't been separated. If I had been a better husband to her, she would never even have been in that dark alley. So you see, it is my fault." His words held such agony that Samantha felt her heart ripping into shreds, her eyes pricking with tears.

"I see no such thing, Will Davenport," she retorted. She could stand it no longer—she took his face in her hands, trying to make him look at her, to see the truth in her eyes.

He groaned and tried to pull away, but she wouldn't let him.

"Do you want to know what I see when I look at you?"

He couldn't answer her. She could practically see the battle that was being fought within him, and she realized that now it was her turn to stand by him, to offer her support, to help him win his war.

"I see a strong man. An honorable man. A man who puts his whole heart into everything he does. A man who puts his daughter's needs above his own. A man who is brave and unselfish."

"I'm not any of those things," he rasped.

"You are in my eyes." She was going to make him hear her, even if she had to put her own heart on the line. She gathered her courage and finished what she'd started to say the other night outside the Grange. "I love you, Will Davenport."

He took a harsh, deep breath, as if someone had punched him in the stomach.

"Samantha, you can't. You shouldn't. I'm not—"

"Why can't you forgive yourself?" she asked before he could finish telling her all the reasons why he was undeserving of love. "God forgives you."

"How can God forgive me?" He shook his head, unwilling to believe it, yet Samantha could see the hope gleaming in his eyes. He wanted to believe. He just didn't know how yet.

"How can God forgive any of us, Will? We've all sinned. No human is worthy of what God gives us. Jesus died so we could have forgiveness. So we could find love."

"Even me?" The hope in his eyes had turned to understanding. She could see the fear receding, replaced by strength and courage. She could see the man she loved coming back to her.

She leaned her forehead against his and reveled in the moment when two hearts became one.

"Even you, Will. Even you."

He framed her face with his large, strong hands, and caressed her cheek with his thumb. "God must have blessed me, if I'm here with you."

He brushed his lips softly against hers, once, and then again.

"Likewise, I'm sure," she whispered against his mouth.

He kissed her again, pulling her close. She could feel the strength of his embrace, yet his touch was infinitely gentle for all that. Tough, yet tender.

When he lifted his head, she had a brief moment of panic. Was he turning away from her again?

But, no. His gaze caught hers, and his mouth

moved as if he were going to speak, but no words came. Not at first.

"You know I'm not a man of words," he said softly, "but these words need to be said. Over and over again. Every day, for the rest of our lives." His eyes glimmered with emotion.

"I love you, Samantha Howell. I want to cherish you. Protect you. And show you every day that I love you."

His smile was radiant. That was the only word Samantha could think to describe it. And it matched the glow of her heart perfectly.

"I love you," he said again, stronger and louder this time. "I love you." The sound echoed through the sanctuary, and he laughed.

He tucked her head against his chest, his cheek resting against her hair. "I love you."

Chapter Fifteen

It was so quiet in the Grange hall that Samantha could have heard a pin drop. It wasn't because the hall was empty. On the contrary, it was full-to-brimming-over with town folks, once again out to support the Howells and Sam's Grocery.

Samantha had taken her place at the front right table, where she'd sat just a week before, facing off against Cal Turner and the Stay-n-Shop legal team. Will sat beside her, his fingers laced with hers. She took a deep, calming breath, and Will squeezed her hand, adding his silent encouragement.

There was no more arguing to be done. The town council had called together this assembly to render their decision. Samantha just hoped she could hear and accept it with strength and dignity. Whatever the outcome, she had Will, her family, her friends and the townsfolk whom she held so dear.

Frank banged his gavel, although why he thought he had to do that was beyond Samantha. No one was speaking. Everyone's attention was already trained on the council.

"I'll come right to the point," Frank said without preamble. "No sense dragging this thing out."

Samantha's heart dropped into the pit of her stomach. If Frank and the council didn't want to draw out the news, it must be bad.

"After much discussion and a thorough review of the issues, we've come to a resolution."

Samantha couldn't help herself. She glanced across the way. Cal grinned and winked, like he was flirting with her. Or rubbing her nose in her pain and loss.

"...Sam's Grocery."

Samantha had been so caught up in Cal's unbelievably callous behavior that she'd missed Frank's pronouncement, but she didn't need him to repeat it.

The crowd cheered. Will stood, pulling her with him as he whooped and turned her around.

"You did it." He kissed her cheek and slid his arm around her shoulders as he turned her to face her exultant family.

"No, Will," she protested, tightening her grip on his waist and meeting his adoring gaze. "*We* did it."

"Hey, you two," Samantha called as Will and Genevieve came in the front door of the store. For some reason she was reminded of the first day Will had walked into her life, hoping he had a job and a place to stay. She knew he hadn't been looking for love—quite the opposite, in fact. But love had found him.

And she was never going to let him go.

"The week is almost up," Will reminded her as he sent Genevieve out back to play with some of the neighborhood children.

His eyes sparkled, and it was then that she realized he was holding something behind his back. His expression didn't reflect his usual serious demeanor. It was light, merry—almost boyish in its enthusiasm.

She smiled. She could get used to this side of Will.

"All right, there, mister. Give it up. What do you have behind your back?"

Why *did* he look that way? What *was* behind his back?

"Wouldn't you like to know?" he teased.

She waited for him to reveal his prize, trying very hard not to imagine the diamond solitaire that Alexis and Mary would have wished for her ring finger. There was time enough for that later. She and Will hadn't even talked through many of the serious issues couples discussed— they were too busy enjoying each other's company for that.

She darted around the counter and made a play for his hand, but he danced back out of her reach.

"Uh-uh. You've got to give me something first."

She reached for the lollipop tub on the counter. "Sucker? I believe I offered you one the first day we met."

He chuckled. "You know that's not what I want. Plant one, right here." He pointed to his cheek. Samantha stood on tiptoe to oblige, but at the last moment turned so her lips landed squarely on his.

"Now then," he continued cheerfully, "I've got something special for you. Something I think you're really going to like."

"Are you going to keep tormenting me, or are you going to show me?"

"I'll show you," he said, bringing his hand out from behind his back.

It wasn't a ring box.

Of course it wasn't a ring box. She was being silly. But she was surprised by the small moment of disappointment that flashed through her. Hopefully it didn't show on her face. The last thing she wanted to do was make Will feel like he'd somehow disappointed her when in fact he just kept exceeding her expectations at every turn. She loved him so much she sometimes thought her heart might burst from it.

She looked closely at what he was holding. It was a small scroll of paper, tied with a red ribbon.

"Let me guess. Is it a Dear John rejection letter? Is it from you?"

"No, it is not," Will denied. "On both counts. And I even tied it with red ribbon because I knew that was your favorite color."

"It was last week," she said with a grin.

"Oh, you ladies. So unpredictable."

"I'll show you unpredictable if you don't give me that paper."

He slipped it into her hand and then crossed his arms, watching with glowing eyes as she pulled the ribbon and rolled the page down flat. She scanned the contents and then squealed in exhilaration and leaped into Will's arms, wrapping her arms around his neck and her legs around his knees.

"It's official!"

"Yes, ma'am. Stay-n-Shop is pulling out of town, and the council is saying good riddance."

Tears pricked at her eyes as joy welled in her heart. Seeing the decision on paper made it final. Certified.

Over.

"I'm going to have to bring you good news more often if I'm going to get thanked liked that," he added, setting her to the floor.

"Just your presence is enough," she assured him.

"Still," he said, "there might be one more surprise for you…"

She narrowed her eyes on him. As far as she could tell, his hands were empty, but his gaze was not. It was full of all the love in the world, and she knew it reflected her own. "One more thing what?" she prompted.

"Well," Will said, reaching into the front pocket of his jeans, "if you insist, I might give you this."

He held up a ring. There was no box, but it was the most beautiful thing she had ever seen.

Or rather, it was the most beautiful moment in the world when Will knelt before her and smiled up at her. He took her hand in his, and she could feel his fingers trembling.

"I want to do this right, Samantha. Starting from this moment." He paused and his lips quirked. "Samantha Howell, will you be my wife?"

She stared first at him, and then at the ring. She would have pinched herself to see if this was real, except the gleam in the depths of Will's brown eyes told her it was true. The diamond solitaire, surrounded by tiny rubies and emeralds, sparkled in the sunshine that poured through the front window.

"Green and red, just in case you change your mind about the color," he teased.

"Oh, you," she exclaimed, holding out her left hand. "Now put that on me."

He stood and wrapped his arms around her waist, then kissed her thoroughly. "I want you to know I love you," he said, his voice deepening with emotion. "I need you with me always. And I promise I'll always have your back."

* * * * *

Dear Reader,

Thank you for embarking with me on a new series once again set in Serendipity, Texas. I'm excited to introduce the Serendipity Sweethearts, otherwise known as the Little Chicks, for those of you who have been following the stories set in Serendipity. These lovely ladies appeared in all of the Email-Order Bride books and are now anxious to have stories (and heroes!) of their own. The first one follows Samantha Howell as she meets strong and silent ex-soldier Will Davenport. He's looking for peace and she's just lost hers, so it's a wild ride for them both to find what they're really after—which of course is true love, both in God and with each other.

I hope you've enjoyed your time with Samantha and Will, and that you'll watch for the next book in the series, which will be Mary Travis's story. You can also find many of my backlist titles available for order from online booksellers in both print and ebook format.

As always, my prayers linger over those who read my books, that they would be a blessing to you in some way. Hearing from you is a great treasure to me. Please email me at debkastnerbooks@gmail.com or leave a comment on my fan page on Facebook. I'm also on Twitter, @ debkastner. Hope to see you online soon!

Keep the Faith,

Deb Kastner

Questions for Discussion

1. Most of us at one time or another feel like David up against Goliath. Relate an experience in which God helped you through what seemed like impossible circumstances.

2. Though he was not related by blood, Will was welcomed into the Howell household as one of their own. What defines a family?

3. Music plays an important part of Samantha's life and worship. How does music touch your life?

4. God often takes what we consider bad situations and turns them to His good purpose. Relate an incident where God took the bad and used it for good.

5. Grandpa Sampson reminded Samantha that there is safety with a multitude of counselors. What does that mean?

6. Will thought he had too dark of a soul to be redeemed. Why is this not true?

7. Why do you think Samantha kept her fight

with Stay-n-Shop to herself, choosing not to involve her family?

8. Do you think building a big-box store in Serendipity would change the town?

9. Who is your favorite character in *The Soldier's Sweetheart*? Why?

10. Samantha prefers to be self-sufficient. She's a giver and not a taker. Is this pride? How do you know the difference?

11. By the end of the novel, Will has accepted the forgiveness of Christ. Was this a sudden conversion, or was it a process?

12. What does Samantha need to learn about herself? What spiritual growth do you see in her throughout the novel?

13. What is the takeaway value of *The Soldier's Sweetheart*? What will you remember the most?

LARGER-PRINT BOOKS!

GET 2 FREE
LARGER-PRINT NOVELS
PLUS 2 FREE
MYSTERY GIFTS

Love Inspired

Larger-print novels are now available...

ReaderService.com

Manage your account online!

- Review your order history
- Manage your payments
- Update your address

*We've designed
the Harlequin® Reader Service
website just for you.*

Enjoy all the features!

- Reader excerpts from any series
- Respond to mailings and
  special monthly offers
- Discover new series available to you
- Browse the Bonus Bucks catalog
- Share your feedback

Visit us at:

ReaderService.com

REQUEST YOUR FREE BOOKS!
2 FREE WHOLESOME ROMANCE NOVELS IN LARGER PRINT
PLUS 2
FREE
MYSTERY GIFTS

✳✳✳✳✳✳✳✳✳✳✳✳✳✳✳✳✳✳✳✳✳✳✳✳✳

HEARTWARMING™

✳✳✳✳✳✳✳✳✳✳✳✳✳✳✳✳✳✳✳✳✳✳

Wholesome, tender romances

YES! Please send me 2 FREE Harlequin® Heartwarming Larger-Print novels and my 2 FREE mystery gifts (gifts worth about $10). After receiving them, if I don't wish to receive any more books, I can return the shipping statement marked "cancel." If I don't cancel, I will receive 4 brand-new larger-print novels every month and be billed just $4.99 per book in the U.S. or $5.74 per book in Canada. That's a savings of at least 23% off the cover price. It's quite a bargain! Shipping and handling is just 50¢ per book in the U.S. and 75¢ per book in Canada.* I understand that accepting the 2 free books and gifts places me under no obligation to buy anything. I can always return a shipment and cancel at any time. Even if I never buy another book, the two free books and gifts are mine to keep forever.

161/361 IDN F47N

Name _____ (PLEASE PRINT)

Address _____ Apt. #

City _____ State/Prov. _____ Zip/Postal Code

Signature (if under 18, a parent or guardian must sign)

Mail to the Harlequin® Reader Service:
IN U.S.A.: P.O. Box 1867, Buffalo, NY 14240-1867
IN CANADA: P.O. Box 609, Fort Erie, Ontario L2A 5X3

* Terms and prices subject to change without notice. Prices do not include applicable taxes. Sales tax applicable in N.Y. Canadian residents will be charged applicable taxes. Offer not valid in Quebec. This offer is limited to one order per household. Not valid for current subscribers to Harlequin Heartwarming larger-print books. All orders subject to credit approval. Credit or debit balances in a customer's account(s) may be offset by any other outstanding balance owed by or to the customer. Please allow 4 to 6 weeks for delivery. Offer available while quantities last.

Your Privacy—The Harlequin® Reader Service is committed to protecting your privacy. Our Privacy Policy is available online at www.ReaderService.com or upon request from the Harlequin Reader Service.

We make a portion of our mailing list available to reputable third parties that offer products we believe may interest you. If you prefer that we not exchange your name with third parties, or if you wish to clarify or modify your communication preferences, please visit us at www.ReaderService.com/consumerschoice or write to us at Harlequin Reader Service Preference Service, P.O. Box 9062, Buffalo, NY 14269. Include your complete name and address.

HWDIR13R

"We were talking about how you needed to learn to accept help from other people."

"And I believe I told you that I didn't need any assistance."

The woman was nothing if not stubborn. She refused to let him help her and her family in this fight, but what she didn't know was that he was at least as stubborn as she was. He *would* help the Howells.

"Once I arrived in Serendipity, you and your family showed me such great kindness. I can never repay you. But I do wish you'd allow me to try. You've already done so much for Genevieve. She thinks the earth revolves around Miss Samantha."

She chuckled and her face brightened. Maybe the world didn't *revolve* around Samantha, but it was definitely made better by her smile.

Will pulled his mental brakes. Whatever was between them didn't matter, because he wasn't going to let it. He was hazardous material and Samantha was too good a person for him to risk wounding her.

She had nothing to gain, and he had nothing to offer. End of subject.

Books by Deb Kastner

Love Inspired

A Holiday Prayer
Daddy's Home
Black Hills Bride
The Forgiving Heart
A Daddy at Heart
A Perfect Match
The Christmas Groom
Hart's Harbor
Undercover Blessings
The Heart of a Man
A Wedding in Wyoming

His Texas Bride
The Marine's Baby
A Colorado Match
*Phoebe's Groom
*The Doctor's Secret Son
*The Nanny's Twin Blessings
*Meeting Mr. Right
†*The Soldier's Sweetheart*

*Email Order Brides
†Serendipity Sweethearts

DEB KASTNER

lives and writes in colorful Colorado with the Front Range of the Rocky Mountains for inspiration. She loves writing for Love Inspired Books, where she can write about her two favorite things—faith and love. Her characters range from upbeat and humorous to (her favorite) dark and broody heroes. Her plots fall anywhere in between, from a playful romp to the deeply emotional. Deb's books have been twice nominated for the *RT Book Reviews* Reviewers' Choice Award for Best Book of the Year for Love Inspired. Deb and her husband share their home with their two youngest daughters. Deb is thrilled about the newest member of the family—her first granddaughter, Isabella. What fun to be a granny! Deb loves to hear from her readers. You can contact her by email at debwrtr@aol.com, or on her MySpace or Facebook pages.